February 1978

ALL THAT GLITTERS

OTHER BOOKS BY NOEL B. GERSON

Fiction

STATE TROOPER
SUNDAY HEROES
DOUBLE VISION
TEMPTATION TO STEAL
ISLAND IN THE WIND
TALK SHOW
CLEAR FOR ACTION
WARHEAD
THE CRUSADER
MIRROR, MIRROR
TR
THE GOLDEN GHETTO
SAM HOUSTON
JEFFERSON SQUARE
I'LL STORM HELL
THE ANTHEM
THE SWAMP FOX
GIVE ME LIBERTY
YANKEE DOODLE DANDY
THE SLENDER REED
OLD HICKORY
THE LAND IS BRIGHT
THE HITTITE
THE YANKEE FROM TENNESSEE
THE EMPEROR'S LADIES
THE GOLDEN LYRE
THE TROJAN
DAUGHTER OF EVE
THE SILVER LION
THE CONQUEROR'S WIFE
THAT EGYPTIAN WOMAN
THE HIGHWAYMAN
THE FOREST LORD
THE IMPOSTOR
THE GOLDEN EAGLE
THE CUMBERLAND RIFLES
THE MOHAWK LADDER
SAVAGE GENTLEMAN

Nonfiction

DAUGHTER OF EARTH AND WATER
THE PRODIGAL GENIUS
BECAUSE I LOVED HIM
FREE AND INDEPENDENT
THE EDICT OF NANTES
P.J., MY FRIEND
FRANKLIN: AMERICA'S LOST STATE
PASSAGE TO THE WEST
SURVIVAL JAMESTOWN
LIGHT-HORSE HARRY
MR. MADISON'S WAR
KIT CARSON
NATHAN HALE
SEX AND THE ADULT WOMAN (WITH ELLEN F. BIRCHALL, M.D.)
BELGIUM: FUTURE, PRESENT, PAST
ROCK OF FREEDOM
SEX AND THE MATURE MAN (WITH LOUIS P. SAXE, M.D.)
FOOD
VALLEY FORGE
THE LEGEND OF POCAHONTAS

All That Glitters

NOEL B. GERSON

Doubleday & Company, Inc., Garden City, New York

Library of Congress Cataloging in Publication Data

Gerson, Noel Bertram, 1914–
All that glitters.

I. Title.
PZ3.G323A [PS3513.E8679] 813'.5'2
ISBN 0-385-08503-6
LIBRARY OF CONGRESS CATALOG CARD NUMBER: 74-4833

PRINTED IN THE UNITED STATES OF AMERICA

For Lin Tai-yi

ALL THAT GLITTERS

I

The heat under the brilliant lights was stifling, in spite of the air conditioning, and the atmosphere in the operating chamber was tense. Members of experienced operating room teams in New York City hospitals supposedly were blasé, but every pair of eyes showing above the face masks reflected a concern that exposed the allegation as a myth.

The anesthesiologist, rhythmically squeezing the rubber bag that pumped oxygen into the patient's lungs, kept simultaneous watch on the instruments that recorded blood pressure and pulse, and maintained a running electrocardiogram. At mid-table, directly above the exposed midsection of the patient's body, two nurses stood ready to hand the surgeon any instruments he might request, while a third hovered behind him, now and then reaching out to mop his forehead so he wouldn't be blinded by his own sweat.

The young resident, who was assisting, tied off small veins with silk thread from time to time in order to keep the bleeding to a minimum, and at the same time observed every move the surgeon made. The operation had already lasted the better part of three hours, and the resident was tired, but he made an effort to conceal his weariness.

Only the surgeon was cheerful, although by rights he should have been exhausted. This was his second long operation of the morning, and by this time other seniors on the hospital staff would have been cursing or barking orders at their subordinates. In the six years Dr. Douglas Gordon had been on the staff, however, no one had ever known him to lose his temper, and he remained unflappable now.

He looked relaxed as he bent over the patient's open abdominal cavity, and the others could hear him humming under his breath. No one had ever been able to distinguish the tune, which was always the same, and it was rumored behind his back that he was tone-deaf. Certainly none of the others could have guessed that his tensions were almost unbearable.

At last he straightened, dropped his scalpel into a tray one of the nurses held out to him, then stretched for a luxurious moment or two. "That does it, Harry," he told the resident. "We'll start closing now."

He used a strong gut thread as he sutured the peritoneum, the membrane that lined the wall of the abdomen, switching to an equally strong thread of artificial substance to bind the muscles. He worked swiftly, as usual, and the other members of the team watched him in silence. He knew what they were thinking, and was pleased that he was known as "the French seamstress," a nickname invented by Army Medical Corps colleagues in Vietnam. Too many surgeons butchered this final phase of an operation because they became careless.

"Take over, Harry," he told the resident as he reached the subcutaneous tissue. "Keep your stitches small, and take your time."

Young Dr. Allen could feel the surgeon's eyes watching every move.

Dr. Gordon yawned behind his mask. "How are things up at your end of the table, Phil?" he asked the anesthesiologist.

"No problems. This guy has the heart and strength of a bull."

"You're rushing, Harry," Douglas Gordon told the resident. "I know you're taking the afternoon off, but your wife will wait the extra five minutes." Even when administering a rebuke his voice remained quiet.

The resident muttered an apology as he slowed his pace.

"That's better. The subcutaneous and the skin need hem-stitching. The lighter your touch the smaller and less obvious the scar." Sensing his subordinate's nervousness, Douglas laughed, then refrained from further comment.

The anesthesiologist added liquid to the IV solution.

Douglas glanced at the clock. "Surgery completed at eleven-thirteen a.m.," he announced to no one in particular. "Ladies and gentlemen, boys and girls, thanks for your help." Not waiting for the patient to be wheeled out, he went to a small dressing room-office in the recovery room area.

There he removed his mask, green gown and cap, peeled off his rubber gloves and washed caked powder from his hands before changing from rubber-soled footgear into his hand-sewn English-made street shoes. The shoes were an extravagance, as were his tailored suit, custom-made shirt and Sulka necktie. But he earned every penny, and was one of the hottest surgeons in New York, with more patients than he could possibly handle. This morning's efforts alone would bring him seven thousand dollars, and he had no one but himself on whom to spend his money. There was nothing wrong with enjoying the symbols of what, for a man still in his thirties, had been a spectacular success.

Before slipping on his jacket he dictated his surgery report, nodding his thanks to the nurse who brought him a mug of black coffee. He grinned at her, but continued to dictate without a break, his sentences concise, and he omitted no vital detail.

Allowing himself the luxury of the day's first cigarette, he reached for the telephone, asked the hospital operator for an outside line and dialed the number he read on a pad before him. "Mrs. Haymaker? . . . Dr. Gordon. Your husband has just been moved to the recovery room from the operating theater, and should regain consciousness in another hour. Take your time coming over, and you'll be waiting for him in his room when they wheel him in. This is just to tell you he came through the operation beautifully. There were no complications, and he should be completely okay after a convalescence that usually runs six to eight weeks. He won't be very chipper for the next few days, but that's to be expected. . . . You're very welcome, Mrs. Haymaker."

Douglas donned a white knee-length hospital coat over his suit, but finished his cigarette and coffee before making his rounds. He had eleven other patients in the hospital, and allotted ample time to each, listening to complaints, answering questions and soothing the sick, to whom his visit was the day's highlight. At no time did he demonstrate impatience or speak in platitudes, well aware that his success was as much due to his attitude as to his skill in the operating room. Patients were people, a maxim he had drilled into himself during his four years of Army service, and he never allowed himself to forget he was dealing with individuals. Not for him the conveyor belt approach to surgery.

His pace quickened at last as he went to the surgeons' day room on the second floor of the new wing and called his office. "I'm just leaving the hospital, Miss Harrell," he said. "I'll be in shortly."

"And high time," someone behind him said.

Even before Douglas turned he recognized the voice of Dr. Edward Baker, his partner. Colleagues jealous of their success attributed their popularity to their charm and good looks, but the pair knew better. Conscientious surgery and meticulous attention to the needs of every individual patient were the principal ingredients that were winning them their following.

"Morning, Eddie. You just arriving?"

"Yep. Our reception room is jammed today."

"Sorry, but I got hung up here. Both cases were tougher than I'd anticipated. I had Haymaker on the table for almost three and a half hours."

Dr. Baker's nod was sympathetic. "The muscle-bound former athletes always take time."

"Where are you headed after you make rounds?"

"I'm teaching a seminar at Columbia today, Doug. And before I forget it, Julie wants you to join us for dinner Thursday. Can you make it?"

"I don't see why not, thanks."

"If you like, Julie will invite a dinner partner for you, but she thinks you might want to bring Eve Harrell."

"I'm tempted, since I drool over her—secretly. But socializing with the hired help can create complications. Is this a party, Eddie?"

"No, just us."

"Well," Douglas said, "as Dorothy Parker once put it, are we getting together for dining or mating? I don't see why I've got to bring a date."

"Julie is suffering from the good woman's syndrome, and wants to see a good friend settle down."

Their eyes met, and although Douglas continued to smile, his expression became guarded. "Sure," he said. "She can make herself happy by getting me a date with one of her friends."

Dr. Baker nodded, but made no reply. There were private areas one did not invade, even when dealing with a partner and former Army comrade. Doug was paying for his mistakes in his own way, and it was his privilege to keep certain aspects of his life hidden behind a wall of reserve.

They parted, and Douglas went directly to the staff lot, where his Mercedes-Benz convertible was parked, and he tried in vain to stop thinking about his conversation with Eddie as he drove to their midtown Park Avenue suite of offices. Julie Baker meant well, but he wished she'd quit trying to involve him in a serious romance. His sex life was active enough to satisfy him, but he had no intention of complicating his existence. If that was what he wanted, Eve Harrell would be happy to oblige. She'd have an affair with him willingly enough, but she was the type who'd begin thinking in long-range terms, which he wanted to avoid. Someday, maybe, if she hadn't found someone else and was still available. But not yet, so he'd continue to walk a tightrope. As only he knew and perhaps Eddie Baker suspected, his options were strictly limited.

He parked in the side street space the Police Department kept for him, entering the office by the back door so he wouldn't have to walk through the waiting room filled with patients. For the next five or six hours he would be examining, consulting, confirming or questioning the diagnoses of the physicians who had referred patients to him. He and Eddie were fortunate, no two ways about it. Virtually all of their practice now came from the referrals made by medical men, which meant most of their patients were genuine surgical cases, and few hypochondriacs wandered in off the street. His career was following the path he had charted for himself in medical school, his accomplishments were solid and he had every reason to be pleased with himself. So it was foolish to allow his brief conversation with Eddie to kick loose an old feeling of restlessness he liked to believe he had conquered.

Eve Harrell, trim in her white uniform, her short blond hair gleaming, appeared to sense his arrival, and came into his office carrying a list of patients waiting to see him. "Good morning, Doctor."

"Hi," Douglas said. "Any four-alarm phone messages?"

She handed him a sheaf of pink slips. "Mrs. Murray called to say that the medication you gave her hasn't killed the pain, and she wants to know if she can increase the dosage. And Dr. Lewis wants to discuss the symptoms of a new patient who is third on the day's list. He wants to be sure you speak to him before you see the patient."

"Okay."

"You're more than an hour behind today, Doctor, so you'll have to move them along." Eve's smile tempered her accusation.

Douglas grinned at her. "Can I help it if I got hung up in surgery? Anyway, you'll needle me until I'm back on schedule."

"Ha!" She knew, just as he did, that he would continue to fall farther behind because he would concentrate his complete attention on each patient who came into his office and would lose all track of passing time. "Do you want to see the mail before the parade begins?"

"Only the important stuff." He reached for the telephone and started to make the more pressing of his calls; he'd squeeze in the others, one or two at a time, between patients.

Eve left the room, very much aware of the fact that his eyes were following her, and returned with a small stack of mail.

Douglas waited until he completed the urgent calls before drawing the pile closer. A cablegram in its distinctive blue-and-white envelope caught his eye, and he opened it first. It had been sent from Hong Kong, and was succinct:

I AM ILL IN ROYAL HONG KONG HOSPITAL STOP NEED YOU DESPERATELY STOP PLEASE COME AT ONCE STOP
ELEANOR CHANG GORDON

He stared at the cable for a long time, his temples pounding, and did not hear the nurse reenter the room.

"Is anything the matter, Doctor?"

Douglas folded the message and placed it in an inner pocket. "What time will Dr. Baker return?"

"He should be here by four."

He removed his jacket and donned a white coat. "I'll start seeing patients," he said, and reached for the case file she had placed beside him.

He worked steadily for hours, trying to devote full attention to each patient, yet unable to put the cablegram out of his mind.

Eve Harrell brought him a mug of coffee while he made several telephone calls during a brief respite. "Do you want me to send out for a sandwich?"

He shook his head. "I'll skip lunch."

"Something you tell patients never to do."

Douglas became irritable. "Don't nag at me, Eve. I know when I'm hungry."

She realized something had upset him, and guessed it had been the cablegram that had disappeared from the pile of mail. But no matter what the cause, he had no right to snap at her when she was trying to protect his health and interests. Sniffing audibly, she turned on her heel.

Douglas became contrite. "Eve."

The nurse hesitated.

"Sorry if I was rude, but this isn't one of my better days."

"I'll order you a corned beef on rye."

He knew better than to argue with her and, rather than become embroiled in a pointless hassle, would throw away the sandwich. "Thanks," he said, "and when Dr. Baker comes in, please tell him I want to see him as soon as possible."

Eddie happened to arrive at a moment when Douglas was between patients, and came straight to his partner's office. "Eve says you're looking for me, and I want a word with you, too. Give me your reaction to these X rays. You're sharper than I am in picking up disorders of the pancreas."

Douglas placed the negatives on his desk. "Eddie, could you fill in for me over the next five to seven days? There are three operations that can't be postponed, and here's a list of patients who must be seen. I'll put the rest on ice. Barring emergencies, these are the only patients who'll need attention."

The request was so unusual, so out of character coming from a man who refused to take vacations, that Baker was startled. "Sure, Doug. What—"

Douglas handed him the cablegram.

Eddie read it, then noted that his partner's eyes had hardened. "I suppose this is authentic."

"I can imagine no reason it wouldn't be." Douglas' voice was unexpectedly stiff.

"What's it all about?"

"You know as much as I do, Eddie. We've had no contact of any kind for years. She's sick, she's in the hospital and she claims she needs me."

"So you'll go to Hong Kong?"

Douglas became bitter. "The way I see it," he said, "I have no damn choice."

II

The only changes in weather in the Mekong Delta came during the monsoon season, when it rained; the heat, which was almost unbearable, was a constant. The year 1966 was different because rain fell during the dry season, too, and Army meteorologists wondered aloud whether the saturation cannonading program instituted by the Field Artillery might be a factor.

Newcomers to the staff of the 124th Field Hospital, and the

group included physicians, surgeons, nurse-anesthetists, nurses and pharmacists, knew only that they lived and worked under nightmare conditions in an inferno. Air-conditioning units that worked had been removed from living and dining quarters and installed in the quonset huts that served as operating chambers. Even Colonel Hale, the hospital commander, had given up the air conditioner in his office so it could be utilized in a quonset hut that was used as a recovery room.

But it wasn't the heat, the insects or the off-duty boredom that most upset the new arrivals. Not even those with long medical experience were prepared for the never-ending stream of casualties brought to the 124th Field for surgery and other treatment. The Cong were clever, no doubt about it, and many of the wounded had been booby-trapped by antipersonnel mines that had ripped off hands and arms, feet and legs. Equally pathetic were the blind, the deaf and the victims of guerrilla sharpshooter attacks, veteran sergeants and teen-aged boys suffering painful abdominal wounds. Cong sharpshooters were particularly adept in firing a single bullet into a man's gut.

From daybreak until nightfall the American artillery roared without stopping, and often the sound grew still louder when fighter-bombers dropped their pay loads on the thick forests of South Vietnam. Even the most timid young medical corpsmen soon became accustomed to the thunder and ignored it.

After nightfall it was the turn of the North Vietnamese and the Viet Cong to retaliate, and the crack of a guerrilla marksman's rifle could cause even veterans of World War II and the Korean War to cringe involuntarily. The gooks possessed the uncanny ability to infiltrate virtually every American military compound, and more than a dozen members of the hospital staff had been killed or wounded in the two years the unit had been in the field.

Only the Chief of Surgery, Major Douglas Gordon, appeared immune to his surroundings. A member of 124th's staff ever since the unit had been sent to the Mekong Delta two years earlier, he ignored American artillery and enemy snipers alike. When casualties were heavy he spent eighteen to twenty hours at a time in surgery, and no one had known him to take a day off. Other surgeons lacked his stamina and determination, and newcomers were privately advised by his deputy and good friend, Major Edward Baker, not to attempt to match his pace.

Fellow physicians who watched him in action for the first time were inclined to agree with the nurses who claimed he had been born without a nervous system. But the old-timers knew better. He had become painfully gaunt, with deep smudges beneath his hazel eyes, and although he was still in his early thirties his brown hair was flecked with gray.

Even when exhausted after spending endless hours in surgery he was incapable of moving slowly, and when he learned the hospital commander wanted to see him he changed without delay from operating room greens to a chino shirt and trousers.

His salute was sloppy.

But Hale, a Regular Army officer and reputedly a martinet, pretended not to notice as he returned the salute and waved the younger man to a chair. "I need to have a little chat with you before you hole yourself up in surgery again." Reaching into a desk drawer, he removed a bottle of Bourbon, and after carefully measuring three fingers of liquor into each of two glasses, he added a small quantity of ice water from a thermos.

"None for me, Colonel," Douglas said. "The helicopters are due to return with another load of casualties soon, and I'll be busy again."

Hale pushed a glass across the desk. "Drink it," he said. "That's an order."

"Yes, sir." Douglas grinned, but left his glass untouched.

"I have here," the Colonel said as he picked up a sheaf of papers, "my recommendation to the theater surgeon general for your promotion to lieutenant colonel."

"Thanks very much." Douglas was indifferent to military rank, so his surprise was genuine.

"God knows you've earned it, so don't thank me. But I want to check out a few angles before I send it along through channels." Hale paused, wondered how to approach his subject with tact, then decided there was no way. "Is it true that the reason you volunteered to spend another two years with the 124th is because your girl sent you a Dear John letter?"

"Eddie Baker ought to be court-martialed and shot. He's the only one out here who has known anything about Betty."

"Major Baker is your friend, and has been worried about you. He isn't alone in his concern."

"Well," Douglas said, "the least he could do would be to get the facts straight. First, I decided to stay on for another two-year tour of duty. I broke the news to the young lady I was intending to marry, but she refused to wait that long and broke the engagement. You heard a backward version of the sequence, Colonel, and it makes a difference."

"A very great difference." Hale raised his glass and stared, waiting for the younger officer to respond in kind.

Douglas had no choice.

"I've never known a more conscientious officer, and I'm curious. Why do you want another tour, Gordon, even if it costs you your girl?"

"At the risk of sounding like a Boy Scout, Colonel, my motives aren't very complicated. This war is kicking up a storm back home, and I have an idea it'll get worse. Whether we ought to be out here, whether the United States should be taking an active military role, is irrelevant from where I sit. I'm an M.D., and my job is healing the sick, alleviating suffering. Regardless of whether our presence in Southeast Asia is right or wrong, *my* presence is right. There's an urgent need for good surgeons in these parts, and I'm damn good."

There was none better, the Colonel thought.

"But don't get the idea that I'm stuffed with nobility," Douglas said. "I'm not. I've got a healthy current of selfishness running through me, too. After two more years of experience at a field hospital in an active combat zone, I'll be ready to tear New York apart in private practice. What I'm learning out here will be worth a mint to me later."

"With your ambitions I'm sure it will," Hale said, sipping his drink. "Provided you live that long."

"I've seen too many casualties to worry about that. If a gook bullet or rocket has my number on it, that'll be that. If it doesn't, I'll carry out my plan."

"I wasn't thinking of the enemy," the Colonel said. "I was referring to your attempt to destroy yourself."

Douglas was startled. "I beg your pardon?"

"You've kept yourself on duty seven days a week, fifty-two weeks a year. No one can keep up that pace, Gordon, not even you. One of these days your hand will slip, and that will be the end of a patient."

Douglas realized he was right, but his nod of agreement was reluctant.

"You've accumulated seven weeks of leave that you haven't taken," Hale said. "What are you trying to prove?"

"It's this way, Colonel," Douglas replied, speaking slowly. "If you'll think back to your own days as an intern and a resident, you'll remember you were tired most of the time, but you slugged through your fatigue. The worst periods were the first few days after you came back from a vacation. You'd lost your rhythm, your whole sense of tempo. Well, that's the way I feel right now. If I ever get out of my present routine, I'm afraid I wouldn't be able to pick up the beat again. Does that make sense to you, Colonel?"

"More than you know, Gordon." Hale leaned forward, placing his elbows on the bare wooden desk. "This is my third war, and I've known more Medical Corps officers than I care to count who have felt just as you do. Few of them have gone to your extremes, but the symptoms have been the same."

Douglas raised an eyebrow. "Symptoms, sir?"

"If you wish, I'll gladly call in one of the psychiatrists to corroborate the diagnosis. You're suffering from an anxiety state brought on by fatigue, and unless you get relief you're headed straight for a breakdown."

Douglas was silent for a moment. "That's a bit hard for me to swallow."

"I've been aware of your condition for some time," Hale said. "I've needed you here, so I've been selfish myself. But I'm responsible for your welfare, and I'd be derelict in my duty if I failed to act as I must. You're taking a furlough for seven weeks."

"I can't!"

"You begin today. Now. So there's no point in spoiling good Bourbon."

Douglas glowered at him, then drained the contents of his glass.

"I'll have the adjutant cut orders sending you to the States, and I'll make sure the surgeon general's office in Saigon books a seat for you on a transport that leaves tonight."

"If you please, sir, I have no reason to go home. My parents are gone, and with my engagement broken off I'd be at loose ends."

"Forgive me for butting in, but I thought you might want to persuade your girl to change her mind."

Douglas shook his head, and his voice became hard. "Not a chance. I'm not blaming her for kissing me off. Four years is a long time to wait for any guy, and she wasn't flattered when I didn't come running back to her after my two years here. But—if she can't understand why I feel compelled to stay, as well as the good it will do my career later—the marriage wouldn't have worked out for me, either."

The Colonel saw he was hurt, and changed the direction of the conversation. "If you don't want to visit the States, there's either Australia or Hong Kong."

"If you're really forcing me to take a furlough I don't want, sir—"

"I am!"

"Then I'll take Hong Kong. I've wanted to go there ever since I was a kid. I don't know a soul in the Colony, and I have no idea what I'll do there for seven weeks—"

"Nothing except loaf, I hope," Hale interrupted. "Go to the beaches, drink more than you should, catch up on restaurants and night clubs and movies. Stay as far away from every hospital in town as you can get, and while you're twiddling your thumbs console yourself with the thought that your promotion to lieutenant colonel will have come through by the time you return to duty."

It was impossible to explain to a Regular that it was the duty itself, not the promotion, that Douglas craved. But the Colonel wasn't the only offender. Betty hadn't understood, either, that he was doing a job as a surgeon, a job that desperately needed to be done, and at the same time was gaining priceless experience.

In spite of the bravura he had displayed he still felt cut up by Betty's rejection, though it was difficult to admit. To hell with her. There were other women in the world, and she had never been his type. Maybe he had proposed to her shortly before leaving for South Vietnam because, as Eddie had insisted, he had tried to establish some sort of link with home.

A heavy rain had fallen, turning the hard-packed dirt roads of the hospital compound into rivers of thick mud that were already caking again under the merciless sun. Walking toward the quarters he shared with his deputy in the officers' self-styled "residential suburb," Douglas told himself that perhaps Colonel Hale was right. He was due for a breather. Lately he'd been forced to exercise great self-control to prevent his hand from shaking when performing surgery, and he was too sound a medical man not to recognize the danger sign.

Major Baker was reading a medical journal in the living room of the quonset hut suite, and lowered the periodical a few inches to peer over the top. "If you're armed," he said, "I'll call the MP's."

"Eddie, you're a bastard!"

"And you're turning into a physical wreck. I couldn't stand aside and watch you fall apart, Doug. What the hell kind of friend would that be? I've never seen anybody more in need of R and R."

"You didn't have to tell the old man about Betty."

"Her rejection has contributed to your mental state. Another missile attack on the hospital, or another of those twenty-hours-in-surgery-without-a-break, and you'd be a prime candidate for a funny farm."

"You'll be delighted to hear I'll be getting out of your hair for seven whole weeks. The adjutant is cutting orders right now, sending me to Hong Kong on leave."

"Ah. Wine, women and song, but not necessarily in that order."

"If that was what I was looking for I could get it in Saigon." There was contempt as well as weariness in Douglas' tone.

"Then what do you want?"

"Nothing. Everything. Damned if I know."

Eddie hesitated. They had been close for eight years, ever since starting to serve their internships together, and he knew that although his friend was developing into a brilliant surgeon, his one weakness was his impulsiveness in establishing personal relationships. "Well," he said, "you've earned your fun, Doug. But be careful. Hong Kong isn't Topeka or Columbus or Trenton."

The military transport circled high above Hong Kong, and from his window seat Douglas could see all of the British Crown Colony below. The outlying area, known as the New Territories, consisted of a broad green belt spread across a chain of hills, and from the air it was impossible to distinguish the border that separated the farming district from Mao Tse-tung's mainland China.

Adjacent to the New Territories and extending to the inner lip of one of the world's most magnificent deep-water harbors was a vast region of urban sprawl known as Kowloon. Here were huge industrial plants and small factories, seemingly endless miles of high-rise slums. Near the Kowloon waterfront, too, were scores of elegant hotels, restaurants too numerous to count and shops selling merchandise of every kind, some of it made locally, some imported from the far reaches of the earth. Douglas had been told that no matter what he might want to buy he would find it for sale in Kowloon.

Beyond the mainland were scattered clusters of islands, some wooded and some populated. The largest of them, directly across the harbor from Kowloon, was that from which the Colony took its name, Hong Kong. One of the most crowded islands on earth, with skyscraper banks and office buildings, apartments and private homes, as well as still more hotels, restaurants and shopping districts, it nevertheless boasted surprisingly large patches of green, many of them public parks.

Douglas oriented himself by checking the actual topography with a map of the Crown Colony, but he was too tired to feel any sense of excitement. Not until the transport landed and he made his way through bustling Kaitak Airport, after going through the formalities of customs and immigration, was he struck by the full impact of Hong Kong.

In South Vietnam most of his time had been spent with hospital colleagues and patients, all of them American. Here, suddenly, he was an alien in the Orient, even though there were obvious ties with the civilization he had known. The blend was curious. Most of the people were Chinese, but wore Western dress, and minis were everywhere. But there were also Indians and Thais, Malaysians and Indonesians, all wearing distinctive national attire.

English was the official language, yet most of the billboard posters and the signs on airport shops were in Chinese. A handful of the newspapers on display were in English, French and German, but at least one hundred were published in Chinese. And sitting at adjacent tables in the open-fronted coffee shop were Chinese eating noodles scooped from wooden bowls with chopsticks and American tourists devouring catsup-smothered hamburgers served with mounds of french-fried potatoes.

Douglas recalled from his undergraduate reading that catsup was a tomato sauce developed in Hong Kong in the mid-nineteenth century to conceal the taste of meat that was turning rancid. The crews of American clipper ships had brought it to the United States, where it had become a staple. That curious historical footnote seemed typical of what he saw around him now. It was his initial impression that Hong Kong was whatever one wanted it to be. In the weeks ahead he would confirm that view.

For twenty-four hours Douglas did not venture out of his hotel, a wooden waterfront structure on the Island that had been taken over by the U. S. Army as an R and R center. At the moment he was interested only in rest, not recreation. He spent most of his time sleeping, arising only long enough to eat a large steak before tumbling into bed again. No sniper fire or thunder of artillery disturbed his slumber, and he heard no sound more menacing than the honking of the horns of the ships of every size and description that sailed in and out of the busy harbor.

Suddenly restless after doing nothing, Douglas went for a stroll on his first tour of exploration. Following the waterfront, he soon found himself in the Wanchai District, the mecca of American and British soldiers, sailors and airmen. Here, crowded into a few square blocks, were scores of sleazy bars and night clubs bearing such names as the New Orleans and the Liverpool, the Leeds and the Baltimore. A glance through the open doors of a few such establishments was enough. Rock music blared, mini-clad B girls beckoned and Douglas fled, knowing he could have found similar dubious delights in Saigon.

A Special Services lieutenant stationed at his hotel directed him to the Officers' Centre, a spacious suite of rooms located on the second floor of a large office building. Taking his time, he wandered from room to room. In the library he saw young men, most of them wearing informal sports attire, reading newspapers flown in from dozens of American cities. In another chamber a number of young ladies, some English and some Chinese, were dispensing tea, coffee and amiable conversation. The visiting officers seemed very much at ease, and Douglas felt out of place.

At last he came to a room identified by a placard as Information Hall, which was dominated by a table on which were piled pamphlets and stacks of mimeographed documents. In each of the four corners was a desk occupied by a young lady apparently prepared to answer questions.

One, a Chinese, was the most beautiful girl Douglas had ever seen. Her blue-black hair fell to her tiny waist, and delicately applied makeup emphasized the regularity of her chiseled features, the liquidity of her dark eyes. Unlike her peers, who were in Western attire, she wore the traditional high-collared *cheongsam*, a tight-fitting dress with a slit on each side of its skirt. He watched her as she carried a paper to the desk of a colleague, and he knew why the style had survived for centuries. She was taller than most of the Chinese he had seen, and the dress brought out every line of her superbly proportioned body.

Douglas waited until she returned to her desk, then approached her. All at once Hong Kong had taken on a new, fresh flavor.

She looked up at him with a warm smile. "Hello, Major. Have you signed the guest book?" Her accent was a pure Oxonian English.

"No, but I'm happy to oblige, if that's the procedure." He took a pen from the breast pocket of his uniform shirt and scribbled his name on a loose-leaf sheet of paper.

"How do you do, Major Gordon? I am Eleanor Chang." She extended a slender hand, and he noted she was wearing a massive gold bracelet and matching ring, both expensive.

"You're westernized." He had no right to pry, but wanted the opportunity to converse with her at length.

"I was born Chang Mei-ling," the girl replied, "Mei-ling meaning little sister, but I changed it when I was baptized. Come along." She led him to the center table and began to hand him various documents. "You'll find this detailed map of both Hong Kong side and Kowloon side useful. This is a catalogue of restaurants by nationality, and this sheet will give you the names and addresses of major churches. This is a list of reliable jewelers and dressmakers if you want to send a gift to your wife—"

"I'm not married."

"And this is a list of the best tailors," she said, absorbing his comment, then marking two of the names. "Neither of these houses will cheat you, and both do good work."

"I wasn't planning on having any clothes made here," Douglas told her.

"How long will you stay in Hong Kong?"

"Well, I've just started a seven-week furlough."

Eleanor Chang became firm. "Then you must buy civilian clothes. Many places automatically charge higher prices when they know they're dealing with a soldier on leave."

"Thanks for the tip. That's good to know."

"And this is a list of our hospitals. If you wish, I'll gladly arrange tours of them for you."

"What makes you think I'd be interested in hospitals?"

She looked at the gold caduceus insignia on his collar. "You're a physician, aren't you?"

"A surgeon. How clever of you to know."

"I should be familiar with your markings. I work here as a volunteer one day a week. But I'd have guessed by looking at your hands that you were a surgeon, a painter or a pianist."

Apparently she was as observant as she was attractive.

The girl returned to her desk, with Douglas beside her. "The Centre operates a volunteer service that may appeal to you. We have many families, in your case that of a local surgeon, who would be pleased to ask you to dinner and guide you around the Colony."

"That's very kind, but I've already found my guide," Douglas said.

"Oh, you have friends here?"

"I'm building a friendship," he replied. "As rapidly as I can. See here, Miss Chang. I intend to go to a great many restaurants in Hong Kong, and I hate to be forced to resort to a process of trial and error to distinguish the good from the bad and the mediocre. The same with performances of Chinese opera, movies, places of special interest like Aberdeen—"

"Ah, you know Aberdeen, Major?"

"I haven't the vaguest idea what or where it is, but I was told I mustn't miss it."

Her laugh was sympathetic.

"I'm not a sight-seer by nature," Douglas said, "but I'll happily go anyplace you think I ought to visit."

She was puzzled by the sudden personal turn the conversation had taken.

"I'm sure you know your way around town, and surely you've eaten at some of the best restaurants."

All at once the girl understood, and averted her gaze.

Douglas warned himself he could frighten her off by moving too quickly. But he very much wanted to see her again and had no intention of waiting for a week until she made her next volunteer appearance at the Centre. "I'll be grateful, Miss Chang, for any time you might be able to spare me while I'm on leave." He was self-confident, but at the same time sounded humble.

Eleanor found the combination appealing, and studied him with care, her face devoid of expression and her eyes opaque.

Only someone familiar with the East would know what she was thinking, Douglas told himself, but his smile did not waver.

"The Centre has no rules that would prevent me from seeing

you," she said at last, "and it happens that I have some time on my hands these days. Yes, Major, I think it can be arranged for me to act as your guide."

III

By the third week of Douglas' stay in Hong Kong he and Eleanor had become inseparable, and he lost count of the days. The war in Vietnam was far away, and only when he saw the haggard faces of uniformed newcomers to Hong Kong did he think of the life he had left behind him and that awaited him on his return to the theater of operations. For the first time in his life he had become a hedonist, relishing the experiences of the moment, and every moment was filled with Eleanor.

He was awakened by the gentle lapping of waves, and a breeze that blew down from the Peak tempered the heat of the scorching sun. Eleanor, clad in a bikini, was stretched out on a blanket beside him, and as Douglas struggled upward through layers of consciousness he remembered they were spending the day at the beach.

They were the only occupants of the crescent-shaped expanse of yellow-white sand, and he marveled at their isolation. Never had he known such an extraordinary place as Hong Kong, and it was difficult to realize that approximately half of the Crown Colony's four and a half million people lived in the immediate vicinity. It was even more difficult to comprehend that three hundred feet behind them, on the far side of dunes studded with palm trees, ran a major highway choked with automobiles, busses and trucks that were driving bumper to bumper.

By walking a short distance from their own car he and Eleanor had managed to cut themselves off from the entire world, and this could be a tiny subtropical atoll, located anywhere on earth, where they were the only inhabitants. The notion was as foolish as it was romantic, and Douglas laughed at himself. Only a short distance from shore he saw a sampan, a distinctive, flat-bottomed boat about fourteen feet in length. A Chinese in nondescript black trousers and shirt sat in the stern, manipulating the tiller, and beneath the semi-covered trestle amidships he could see a shabby woman washing clothes in a bucket. Several children were playing near the sharp-pointed prow, and it occurred to Douglas that the entire family probably knew no other home.

Farther from shore and heading toward Hong Kong Harbor was a junk returning to port after several days of fishing in the South China Sea. This large vessel, which could carry a crew of as many as twenty men, was unique in appearance, too, with a high poop, battened lugsails and a prominent stem. Ungainly at first sight, she nevertheless rode in the water with easy grace, and for thousands of years had proved there was no more seaworthy ship afloat. Again laughing under his breath, Douglas reflected that by no stretch of the imagination could this be Cape Cod or Fire Island.

But it was the proximity of Eleanor, more than all else combined, that reminded him he was in Hong Kong. This loveliest of girls had become the symbol of this most fascinating of all places. Propping himself on one elbow, he looked at her as she napped, and told himself only idiots believed members of his profession were immune to the attractions of the human body. Eleanor was the most graceful creature he had ever known, and he took in every detail of her gently sloping shoulders and high breasts, long torso and flat stomach, rounded hips and slender legs.

She was the personification of all that was feminine and desirable, and he wanted her so badly he had to fight hard to curb an urge to take her here and now. She was a lady, and had spent the better part of her life in the Orient, so she well might react negatively to a brusque demonstration of Western violence. The very idea of not being able to see her again was unbearable.

Douglas forced himself to face his situation squarely. Eleanor was ever-present in his mind, regardless of whether they were together or apart, and by every criterion he knew he had fallen in love with her. Eddie would tell him he was moving too fast, and Douglas knew all the arguments. He had worked himself into a state of exhaustion in a combat zone and was overreacting to beauty, warmth, charm and sympathy. He was exaggerating Eleanor's assets because she was the first woman he had known well in two years, other than the prostitutes he had visited at officers' brothels on brief trips into Saigon. And he was very much on the rebound after Betty had rejected him.

Common sense told him he knew too little about Eleanor to feel much more than a surface attraction to her. His actual knowledge of her background consisted of small scraps of information and large conjectures. She lived alone in a small but handsomely furnished flat, she dressed well and she drove a Jaguar convertible, so he assumed her family had left her fairly well fixed, particularly as she held no job. But he merely assumed her parents were dead; she had never discussed them.

He also guessed her upbringing had been genteel because she was the complete lady. And she must have received a solid education because she could discuss Western as well as Oriental literature, art, music and drama, and was conversant with world affairs. From a comment she had made at dinner the other evening he had concluded that she had attended school in England for several years, but that, too, was a mere assumption. Common sense told him to slow down.

To hell with common sense. He was falling in love with her, no question about it.

Eleanor stirred beneath his gaze, opened her eyes and smiled up at him.

He could no longer resist the invitation, and bent down to kiss her.

Her lips were full and moist, and she responded eagerly; in a few moments she was trembling.

Douglas slid his arms around her and drew her closer.

Suddenly the girl pushed him away. "There's a hairpin curve on the road cut into that high hill about one hundred and fifty yards from here. Anybody making the turn can see us easily, and Hong Kong truck drivers are susceptible to suggestions of romance. We don't want to be responsible for a bad accident!"

"At the moment," Douglas said, his voice hoarse, "I couldn't care less."

Eleanor laughed as she jumped to her feet. "I'll race you to the raft and back!" she cried, and began to run toward the sea.

She was more quick-footed than he had realized, and it took him a few moments to regain his equilibrium, so she reached the water's edge a step ahead of him. They continued to run, kicking up sprays of salt water, until they were thigh-high. Then they plunged in, and as Eleanor dove beneath a wave, her crawl stroke long and powerful, Douglas realized she was racing in earnest. His own spirit of competition flared, and he made an effort to overtake her. In spite of his greater strength, however, she was the better swimmer, and she maintained a lead that stretched to more than three yards by the time they splashed through the shallows and ran back to their beach blankets and picnic baskets.

They were laughing and breathless when they halted, and Eleanor was so lovely that Douglas took a step toward her.

A subtle change in her expression indicated that this was not the time or place for a demonstration of affection. "Here," she said, handing him a towel, "we must dry off and be on our way. We'll barely have time to change if we intend to reach the restaurant in Aberdeen just as the moon rises."

He knew her attitude was both correct and sensible, but his urge to embrace her was in no way lessened. The understanding in her eyes tempered his disappointment, however, and he promised himself that tonight they would have a serious talk. He could wait no longer.

They circled Hong Kong Island on the forty-five-minute drive to Aberdeen from the city proper, with Eleanor, clad in a sleeveless cocktail dress, behind the wheel of her Jaguar. For a time she played the role of a guide, pointing out a famous old resort hotel, the estates of various shipping, banking and mercantile magnates, several old, crumbling forts and public parks that stood adjacent to concrete and glass apartment buildings. But Douglas concentrated on her rather than the scenery, and after a time she fell silent. A tension previously lacking in their relationship was becoming evident.

Aberdeen, a fish-processing and manufacturing city of about a hundred thousand, was a solid mass of people, all of whom seemed to be strolling through the narrow streets as they bought food, items of clothing, hardware and pharmaceutical supplies in tiny open-fronted shops located on the ground floors of ten- and fifteen-story tenement buildings. Douglas had been struck by the vast numbers of people he had seen on the streets of both Hong Kong and Kowloon sides at any hour of night or day, but Aberdeen seemed even more crowded, and Eleanor drove at a crawl.

She parked the convertible several blocks from the waterfront, and the press of humanity was so great that Douglas took her hand so they wouldn't be separated in the throng.

He started to clear a path for her, but she tugged at his hand. "We're in no hurry," she said. "We'll move with the tide."

Douglas thought it fortunate he didn't suffer from claustrophobia as he looked out at the sea of men in short-sleeved shirts and trousers, older women in house dresses and girls in miniskirts. Every inch of space on the tarred road was occupied, and there were no sidewalks anywhere, all the way to the waterfront.

Gradually it occurred to Douglas that the crowd, good-natured in the main, was hostile to him and to Eleanor. No one spoke to them or made an even vaguely threatening gesture, but as people gazed at the couple, then looked away with eyes suddenly blank, he became increasingly certain they were expressing their disapproval, with a subtlety of which only Orientals were capable. He had come into enough contact with the East in Vietnam to have picked up a few fundamentals about this part of the world.

Perhaps the people of Aberdeen were resentful because he and Eleanor were better dressed, or because of her low-cut neckline. Ethnic Chinese, regardless of nationality, sometimes displayed curious Puritanical tendencies.

Suddenly Douglas realized the truth. He was a Caucasian, perhaps the only one in Aberdeen at this particular moment, and in the experience of these poverty-stricken Orientals a white man went out with a Chinese girl for only one reason. He felt his face growing warm, and he wanted to shout they were mistaken: differences in race meant nothing to him, Eleanor was unique and he felt increasingly positive that he wanted to marry her.

He could say nothing to these strangers, of course, but it was imperative that he make his intentions clear to the girl herself tonight. And if she wanted to terminate their relationship when she learned what he had in mind, well, that was a risk he'd have to take.

The couple spent almost a quarter of an hour making their way to the waterfront, and Eleanor led her companion to a dilapidated dock festooned with strings of green, orange and blue lights. Many of the bulbs were burned out, Douglas noted, and Eleanor had to walk with care so her heels wouldn't catch in the gaps between the boards.

At the end of the dock stood a sampan, similarly decorated, and Douglas helped the girl step aboard. They seated themselves amidships in old chairs of woven bamboo, and a frail white-haired woman in rusty pajamas began to scull the little craft across the water. She looked too old to perform the task, but her strength was deceptive, and the sampan moved quickly toward the outer part of the harbor.

"I promised you a moon," Eleanor said. "There it is."

A huge yellow ball appeared on the horizon, and immediately began a slow ascent. The old woman threaded a path between towering junks that rode at anchor, and the scene reminded Douglas of a stylized painting of the Far East. Never had he felt so alien.

His sense of unreality increased when he looked off to his right and saw endless rows of sampans jammed together hull to hull. These, he had read, were the homes of about a hundred thousand so-called "boat people." The men found occasional work going to sea on the junks, but the women reared their families and spent virtually their entire lives on their tiny cramped homes, rarely going ashore and buying the necessities of life from itinerant peddlers who also lived on boats.

Reality returned when Douglas wondered how so many could survive under such unsanitary conditions. No wonder the Hong Kong health authorities were appalled and were exerting every effort to persuade the sampan dwellers to move into new facilities being built for them in Aberdeen.

The old woman cleared a cluster of junks, and the floating restaurant loomed ahead. It stood four decks high, with a pagoda roof and a carved dragon prow; strings of bright lights brought out the details of its gold- and silver-painted hull, which resembled the walls of an ancient temple. Here was the romantic China of storybook illustrations, so conspicuous by its absence in Hong Kong, a city of modern utilitarian buildings that had not been founded until the middle of the nineteenth century.

The moon helped bring out every detail of the huge floating restaurant, and Eleanor was bathed in its soft light, too. Douglas looked at her and promptly put the medical problems of the boat people out of his mind.

The couple received a ceremonious welcome, and were escorted to a tank, where Eleanor selected the fish that would be poached for their first course. Then they were seated at a railside table in the open, with the moon's glow flooding Eleanor's lovely face.

They were served excellent cocktails, and as they sipped the iced drinks Douglas began to talk about his future. "I've agreed to spend two more years in Vietnam," he said, "and so has my deputy. Then we're going to open our own practice in New York."

"Why New York?" Eleanor asked. "America is such a large country that many other places must need doctors more than New York."

"There are more poor there than anywhere else, and more rich people, too. I want to serve humanity, but at the same time I want to make a lot of money. Before my parents died they made a great many sacrifices to send me to medical school, and I want their efforts to have been worthwhile."

"To me," she said, "a desire for wealth is a legitimate ambition. Which can only be appreciated by those who have known hunger."

"You've been poor, too?"

Eleanor smiled, but made no reply.

"Surgery," Douglas said, "is the only profession I know that can satisfy both my conscience and my yen for a big bank account."

"You are good at your work?"

"Yes, and I'm getting better all the time," Douglas said. "I'm not boasting, which would fool no one. A scalpel doesn't lie, and by the time I get to New York I'll be able to hold my own with any top surgeon."

"Have you thought of opening a practice here?" she asked.

He was surprised. "In Hong Kong?"

"There are many rich here, and very many poor, too."

Douglas shook his head. "I'd have to take special examinations to get my license, and I'd always be an alien because I wouldn't give up my American citizenship. But there's an even more important reason. I'd be out of the mainstream. It wouldn't be enough for me to become one of the leading surgeons in a place like Hong Kong. I've got to be a big frog in the main pond. And to my way of thinking that's New York, no other place."

"You're right when you say you're ambitious. I've known few men who want so much."

"Is that bad?"

"No, of course not!" Eleanor leaned forward, speaking earnestly. "I think it's wonderful. If I were a man I'd feel exactly as you do."

Her approval enabled him to breathe more easily, but he wanted to lead gradually into what he had in mind, so he kept his tone light. "What do you want for yourself?"

"Oh, my goals aren't unusual."

"For instance."

"A happy marriage and home. And comfort. I must have comfort. It would drive me mad if I had no money."

"So it's a good thing your family keeps you supplied with funds." His probe was delicate.

"Like you, I have no family." Eleanor volunteered no details.

"But you have enough," he persisted.

"How much is enough?" There was amusement in her shrug. "I manage, but I can't say I'm satisfied. If I own twenty dresses I want forty. If I own one car I want two. There is an old Peking legend that fits me, I think. Once there was a man who worked very hard so he could build a new room onto his cramped house. No sooner did he build it than he wanted another. And yet another. Finally he had a house so big it had more rooms than he and his sons and his grandsons could use. By the time he discovered his mistake he was very old, and it was too late."

Douglas wondered whether she and her family had come to Hong Kong as refugees from Peking. Only the northern Chinese were tall, and something in her manner seemed to set her apart from local people, too. "Do you know Peking?"

"I first heard the story when I was little." Her reply was evasive, but she smiled warmly.

He was intrigued by her talent for turning aside questions, but at the same time he was eager to learn more of her background. "In the three weeks we've known each other," he said, "you've told me almost nothing about yourself."

"There is so little to tell." Eleanor remained enigmatic. "The past is always boring. I live in the present, for the future, and I am what you see."

He knew as little about her present as he did about her past, and it occurred to him that she hadn't introduced him to one of her friends. Perhaps she was holding him at arm's length until they became even better acquainted, so he warned himself not to propose marriage prematurely. A full month of his furlough remained, so he needn't rush.

The waiter brought another round of drinks, and as Eleanor raised her glass her eyes met his.

If romantic love was the curse of Americans, Douglas was delighted to be cursed. Overwhelmed by his feelings, he followed the girl's example and forgot everything but her proximity at this very moment.

Awakening gradually, Douglas realized his furlough would end in seven more days, and he wanted to spend every minute of that time with Eleanor. He started to climb out of bed, then saw the surroundings were unfamiliar and paused. Eleanor was asleep beside him, and he remembered this was her apartment, not the officers' R and R hotel.

Last night had been the first they had spent together, and a feeling of tenderness welled up in him as he looked down at her. After a month and a half of self-denial their lovemaking had been spontaneous and explosive, and every aspect of their union had been perfect. Best of all, Douglas felt certain Eleanor returned his love. She had given of herself so joyously, so freely, that he knew she felt as he did.

Perhaps he had punished and deprived himself unnecessarily by waiting as long as he had, but that was a short-sighted view. He hadn't been seeking a quick affair, and the restraint he had exercised for weeks would pay dividends now.

Eleanor stirred, opened her eyes and smiled up at him. "What a wonderful way to wake up," she murmured.

He greeted her with a lingering kiss, then drew back. "No regrets?"

"None. I've never been so happy. What about you?"

He turned away from her for a moment and reached into the inner pocket of his folded jacket, which lay on a chair beside the bed. Removing a small box, he opened it for her inspection.

Eleanor's dark eyes shone as she saw the gold ring set with rubies and diamonds. "You're very wicked, Douglas. This cost you a fortune!"

"I'll earn far bigger fortunes."

"When—"

"Yesterday, while you were having your hair done. I had planned to get you a solitaire, but you admired this in a window one afternoon last week, and I made up my mind then that you'd have it. The only problem was finding the right shop again. This whole town is one big jewelry store, and I must have gone to a dozen places before I came across it."

The ring continued to fascinate her. "I can't let you spend all your money on me."

"You can't stop me." He took the ring from the box and slipped it onto the fourth finger of her left hand.

"It fits!"

"Of course. I borrowed one of your rings the other day when you took off several before we went swimming. The jeweler changed the size in no time."

"You think of everything."

"Where you're concerned, I try," he said.

They embraced, pressing close, and their desires, satiated the previous night, were reawakened. That intimacy had given them greater mutual understanding, and they cast aside all reserve, any lingering awkwardness or shyness disappearing. Aware of the ecstasy that awaited them, they hungered for it, their memories sharpening their erotic appetites.

But Douglas was in no hurry, so he slowed the pace, wanting to prolong their pleasure. Also, he knew, this was the right psychological moment to raise the question he had waited for weeks to ask.

"Will you marry me?" His voice sounded husky in his own ears.

Eleanor's reply was so soft he could barely make out her words. "Ask me again—in an hour," she said, and submitted to his lovemaking.

IV

The jumbo jet circled above Kaitak Airport, awaiting its turn to land, and Douglas, looking out of the window, was astonished by the changes that had taken place in Hong Kong during the six years that had passed since he had last seen the Crown Colony. The factory area on the Chinese mainland was expanding, and cut deeply into the New Territories, vastly reducing the farm acreage there. Hong Kong and Kowloon sides each boasted a dozen or more new skyscraper office buildings and hotels, and only the harbor, filled with hundreds of passenger vessels and freighters, tankers and junks, sampans and the many white, double-decker ferries that sailed in crisscrossing patterns, was the same.

The terminal building had been enlarged, Douglas discovered after his aircraft landed, but the crowds were no less dense. The chilled air was as stale in the mid-1970's as it had been in the late 1960's.

"Welcome to Hong Kong," the immigration inspector said, stamping Douglas' passport. "Enjoy your holiday, Doctor."

"Thanks a lot." Douglas' voice was dry.

The uniformed agents of the Preventive Service, which performed customs duties, were still cheerful and efficient. The young Chinese officer behind the counter made a thorough but swift examination of Douglas' luggage, then summoned his supervisor, an Englishman wearing a Sam Browne belt and the insignia of his rank on his shoulder boards. They conferred briefly, and the supervisor came to Douglas.

"Sorry to hold you up, Doctor, but I'm told you're carrying a small quantity of drugs in your hardware kit."

"I take my medicine bag everywhere with me," Douglas said. "Force of habit, I guess. If you want to hold the morphine and anything else you may find questionable, just give me a receipt for them and I'll pick them up when I leave Hong Kong."

"May I see your credentials?"

Douglas handed the Englishman his passport and the hospital passes of three New York institutions.

The supervisor looked at them, then returned them with a smile. "I see no need to impound your supplies, Doctor. Enjoy your holiday here, sir!"

Hong Kong officialdom, it appeared, couldn't imagine an American would come to the Colony for any reason other than a vacation.

Traffic was so heavy in the Kowloon business and shopping district that Douglas drummed impatiently on the window ledge of his taxi. But a pleasant surprise awaited him. Instead of depositing him at the Star Ferry for a leisurely boat ride to Hong Kong side, the driver took him through the new four-lane tunnel that had been built beneath the harbor.

Less than five minutes later Douglas was deposited at one of the new hotels, where he had made a cabled reservation. He registered, but was not in too great a hurry to go to his room, so he had his luggage sent upstairs and returned to the entrance for another taxi.

The crowds that filled the streets were no less dense than they had ever been, Douglas realized absently. And he couldn't help wishing Eleanor had suffered her crisis at some season other than early summer, when the subtropical heat was suffocating.

The taxi moved past the official residence of the Governor, and Douglas felt sorry for the Gurkha guards standing at attention outside twin sentry boxes. Their uniforms were of heavy wool, and it was a medical miracle that soldiers on duty there weren't felled regularly by heat prostration.

The Royal Hong Kong Hospital consisted of several buildings clustered on a campus behind a five-foot stone wall. Douglas guessed it was a thousand-bed institution, and he noted, without realizing it, that the operating rooms were located on the second floor of the main building.

Visiting hours for the day hadn't yet started, a lobby sign told the American, and a Chinese nursing sister in crisp white looked at him in open disapproval.

He handed her his card. "I'm here to see Eleanor Chang Gordon," he told her.

"Is she a private or state patient?"

"I have no idea."

"One moment, Doctor." She rummaged through several card files, then turned back to him. "I'm sorry, but we have no patient registered under that name."

He had no intention of allowing administrative red tape to thwart a mission that had brought him halfway around the world. It appeared that hospitals everywhere were crippled by the inefficiency of people who didn't know their jobs. Certainly he would not become embroiled in an argument with an underling. "I'd like to see the matron in charge of admissions, please," he said.

The nursing sister heard the authority in his voice, and after a moment's hesitation disappeared into an inner office, then came into the open again and beckoned.

The uniformed Chinese matron, wearing two black bands on her starched white cap, resembled many head nurses Douglas had known, and the severity of her manner did not awe him. "I understand you're seeking a patient who isn't registered here, Doctor."

"I'm sure she was here thirty-six hours ago. If she isn't using the name of Eleanor Chang Gordon, try either Eleanor Chang or Chang Mei-ling."

The matron went into the outer office and made a thorough search of the card files.

Douglas watched her through the open door, and as she returned her expression told him he had come to Hong Kong on a wild-goose chase.

"We've had no patient under any of the names you've mentioned, not in the past year," she said. "I've gone through the files personally, and I assure you they're accurate."

He was bewildered and his heart sank, but he held his ground. "I hate to be a nuisance, but I'd appreciate a few minutes of the Director's time."

The matron sniffed as she vanished down a corridor.

Douglas knew he might be suffering a sense of displacement caused by his travel through so many time zones, but he hadn't gone insane. Eleanor's cablegram was in his pocket, and was real. He was sure of that much, no matter what the hospital records indicated.

The matron returned, her manner stiff. "Dr. Wong will see you," she said, and led him to a large office at the end of the corridor.

A short, slender Chinese in a white coat rose from a chair behind his desk, Douglas' card in one hand. "Welcome to Hong Kong, Doctor. I'm Dr. Wong."

"Thank you, Doctor, and for letting me interrupt you."

"Not at all. I spent two years as a resident at New York Hospital many years ago, and had the honor of working under Edgar Miller." Wong waved his visitor to a chair.

Douglas felt a wild surge of impatience, but professional amenities had to be observed. "I met him only once, two years ago, when he called me in consultation on a rather complicated thyroidectomy. But I never had the pleasure of seeing him at work in the operating room."

The Chinese sighed. "It was surgery's loss when he suffered a coronary last year. I don't suppose you've heard whether there's been a recurrence."

"The last I heard, he was living in Sarasota and playing eighteen holes every day."

Again the Director sighed, then remembered his manners. "May I offer you some tea?"

"No, thank you, Dr. Wong. I'm anxious to get to the bottom of something that mystifies me." Douglas reached into his wallet and handed the cablegram across the desk.

The slender man read it several times.

Douglas laced his hands together so he wouldn't drum on the desk.

"This is very odd, Dr. Gordon," the Chinese physician said. "I assure you Matron Teng is reliable, and I think it unlikely that she erred."

Douglas nodded, his mind whirling. He could imagine no reason why Eleanor would have summoned him to Hong Kong without cause, and if someone else had played a practical joke on him—for reasons unknown—it was a vicious trick.

Dr. Wong was lost in thought, and stared out of the window at a gnarled pine tree that looked like a picture postcard of a Chinese garden.

Douglas wondered whether the man had forgotten his presence, and didn't know how to make his excuses and leave without sounding too abrupt.

Suddenly Dr. Wong picked up a telephone and spoke rapidly in the Mandarin dialect.

Eight years earlier Douglas had begun a study of Chinese, but after his permanent return to the United States he had abandoned the effort, and could understand no more than an occasional word.

The Director replaced the telephone in its cradle, and realizing his visitor was badly upset, made his manner professionally soothing. "We won't give up hope just yet. My secretary is checking with the mail desk to see if any messages were left there for you."

"Thank you." The American thought of the time he had lost, the money he had spent, the extra work he had piled onto the shoulders of his partner.

"I hope," Dr. Wong said, "you'll find time to have lunch with me while you're out here. You may want to visit our surgery—some of our techniques are rather advanced, I'm pleased to say. And our use of acupuncture as an adjunct to standard practices of anesthesia may be new to you."

"That would interest me very much." Douglas was too disturbed to think in professional terms.

A young Chinese woman in a snug-fitting minidress came into the room, and in one hand she carried a sealed envelope.

Douglas' temples pounded.

The secretary ignored the presence of the visitor, and saying a few words in Mandarin to the Director, handed him the envelope.

Dr. Wong glanced at it, then passed it across the desk. "Your troubles are ended, Dr. Gordon."

Douglas saw that his name had been printed on the envelope with a felt-tip pen, and in the lower left-hand corner was the notation, *Please hold pending arrival.* Not bothering to excuse himself, he tore it open.

The communication, which lacked both a salutation and a signature, bore the previous day's date, and the hand-printed message was brief:

> *I have no idea when or if you'll come to Hong Kong, but I am writing this in the hope you will see it. I pray, for the sake of the past, that my cablegram will bring you to me.*
>
> *Do you remember our favorite place to watch the sun set? I'm sure you do.*
>
> *Each afternoon for the next week I shall be there at 4* P.M.*, and shall wait thirty minutes for you to meet me.*
>
> *Please, please—don't fail me! I am desperate, and only you can help me.*

"There, you see," Dr. Wong said. "You were upset without cause, Dr. Gordon."

"So I was." Douglas saw no point in revealing his suspicion that his troubles were just starting. But he had to say something to take care of the discrepancy between the cablegram and the letter. "It appears the lady was the victim of a misunderstanding," he said lamely. "Either she didn't understand her physician's diagnosis or he changed it. I'm being asked to consult with him today, and I'm sure everything will straighten out."

"Quite so," Dr. Wong said, too polite to indicate he didn't believe a word of the tale.

Thanking him again, Douglas promised to return for a visit to the operating rooms when time permitted, and a few minutes later he was seated in a taxi that took him back to his hotel. As an intern he had learned to sleep anywhere, under any circumstances, so he hadn't done too badly on the long direct flight from New York.

But he was in need of a shower, a shave and a change of clothes. He was ravenous and, now that he thought about it, he could use a stiff drink, too. It was only 11 A.M., local time, so he had hours to kill before meeting Eleanor.

As nearly as he could judge, she was suffering from no ailment of any kind and had lied in her cable, knowing that nothing else would have impelled him to come to Hong Kong. Her trickery had made him look foolish in the eyes of a colleague, and he didn't intend to forgive her for that, either. In fact, he was tempted to head straight back to New York on the next flight.

He knew, however, that he wouldn't. He was curious about Eleanor's elaborate subterfuge and her reasons for wanting to see him. Most of all, he was curious about her. Six years was a long time, but he hadn't forgotten her, not by a damn sight.

Staring out of his twentieth-floor hotel room window at the perpetual motion in the harbor below, he remembered everything about her, including details he had gone to great pains to put out of his mind. He would be wise, he supposed, to consign her to his past and not let her intrude on his present. But he forced himself to face the truth, and had to admit he hadn't been able to get her out of his system.

Like it or not, she was still his wife.

He had married her a few days before his furlough ended, in a ceremony performed in one of the small chapels in the Anglican Cathedral. Thereafter he had obtained leaves of a few days at a time whenever he could be spared from his duties at the hospital, and had paid her eight or nine visits during his two-year tour. He had arranged with the Army to pay her the bulk of his lieutenant colonel's salary, and she became a major factor in his plans for the future. Not only would she fit into his life as a New York surgeon, but would give him a social distinction that would enable him to stand apart from others.

As he learned much later, Eddie Baker had disapproved of the marriage from the outset, an opinion that hardened after Eddie made it his business to go to Hong Kong on leave for the express purpose of meeting Eleanor. Realizing that nothing he might say would reverse an accomplished fact, he had kept his views to himself.

In retrospect Douglas could see that trouble began to develop about six months before his tour in Vietnam ended. Eleanor responded vaguely to his specific proposals regarding their joint move to New York, but at the time he failed to recognize her evasiveness. Not until he reached Hong Kong on his way back to the United States did he awaken to what was in store, and he was sure he would always remember everything that had taken place in Eleanor's flat. . . .

"We'll spend a couple of days at a San Francisco hotel while I go through the red tape of being relieved from active duty," Douglas said. "Then we'll fly straight to New York, and you can hunt for a place to live while I have my talks at the hospitals. As I wrote to you, I've been corresponding with several, and the staff openings at a couple of them sound interesting."

Eleanor made no reply, and seemed to be concentrating on a table ornament, a carved jade slab that she brushed with the tips of her slender fingers.

He continued to wander around the half-familiar living room of her flat. "Have you picked up your visa at the U. S. Consulate General yet?"

She shook her head.

Douglas curbed his annoyance. "I wrote you about it specifically. I told you to take them a copy of our marriage license when you made your application. I'd better go in with you—this morning—to make sure no snags develop. I don't expect any problems, but these things can eat up time."

Eleanor slipped the jade slab into its stand and faced him. "I've written to you many times, too, and I wish you'd consider my advice."

"I know you've been urging me to set up a Hong Kong practice, and I've thought about it. I really have. But there are too many obstacles. I'd have to be a resident here for twelve months before I could even take a medical practitioner's examination. I already hold a New York license, and I can go to work there without delay. Besides, I'm an American citizen, and my whole future is there."

"Hong Kong," she said, "is my home."

"We'll go to work on your U.S. citizenship as soon as your permanent residence visa is granted."

Eleanor stood. "I want to stay here. As a subject of the Crown."

The full import of what she was saying struck Douglas, and he could only stare at her.

"We could be happy together right here," she said. "There's a need for good surgeons in our hospitals."

"I've already explained to you that my place is in New York," he said, his voice rising.

"Then you'll have to go without me." Her face was set.

"Why, for God's sake?"

"Intermarriage is accepted here. On our level of society."

"It'll be accepted in the States, too! Besides, as long as it doesn't matter to us—"

"I prefer not to take that risk," she said, her voice firm.

Douglas' eyes narrowed. "Are you looking for an excuse to break up our marriage? If you are, you've chosen one hell of a flimsy way out!"

Eleanor remained calm. "If you decide to stay here, I'll live with you as your wife until the end of our days. But if you insist on going to America, you'll go alone. I want no money or property, and I won't fight you if you want a divorce."

The future on which he had been planning was collapsing, and he became frantic. "I think you've gone crazy!"

"You've been working very hard at the hospital in South Vietnam," Eleanor said, still resolute, "while I've been sitting here, doing very little except thinking. I know our marriage would fail in New York, or anywhere else in the States. You'd try, and so would I, but trying wouldn't be enough, and it would be senseless to waste all that effort and time. Stay here, and I know we can make a success of our relationship. If you must go, you'll go alone. I won't blame you for hating me, although I hope you won't. And I promise I won't think any less highly of you."

V

Traffic on Hong Kong's Connaught Road was as heavy as that in Manhattan at rush hour, Douglas told himself as he tried to relax in the taxi that was carrying him to his rendezvous with Eleanor. Private cars and trucks barely inched forward, cramming the street bumper to bumper, but there was no sign of the rickshaws that, until recently, had added such a colorful touch to the Crown Colony's ambiance. Virtually every building was a glass, chrome and cement skyscraper, and only because virtually all of the pedestrians who overflowed the sidewalks were Chinese did the visitor know he was in the Orient rather than a modern American city. The growth of Hong Kong during the six years he had been away was phenomenal, and the combination of the strange and the familiar made him uncomfortable.

He knew, however, that the real reason he was fidgeting was because he would see Eleanor again, and under circumstances in which she obviously wanted his help. In his one candid discussion of his domestic situation with Eddie Baker, his partner had insisted he hadn't divorced Eleanor because he was still in love with her, still hoped that a miracle of sorts would bring her to his side in New York.

Douglas had denied the charge, saying he had refrained from obtaining a divorce because he had been too busy to bother, particularly as he had found no one else he wanted to marry. Certainly he wasn't carrying a torch for a woman of whom he thought infrequently and whom he hadn't seen in six years. All the same, he couldn't help wondering whether there might be some small germ of truth in Eddie's claim. Eleanor had made an indelible impression on him, and he had found no one to take her place. But he wouldn't have made the long journey to Hong Kong had he known she wasn't critically ill, as her cablegram had alleged, and he intended to tell her what he thought of her shabby trick.

The taxi successfully negotiated the Wanchai District, and traffic lessened as it headed into a residential area of private homes and de luxe apartment houses. It headed inland, and soon deposited Douglas at the front gate of an amusement park unlike any other on earth.

Tiger Balm Garden had been the gift of a patent medicine manufacturer to the people of Hong Kong, and admission to its grounds and buildings was free. A dozen or more pavilions built in the traditional pagodalike Chinese style of architecture were scattered in an immaculately tended subtropical park. Grotesque figures of animals and humans, most of them resembling cartoons, were on display in the various structures, and gave substance to the claim that Tiger Balm was an Oriental Disneyland.

Entire families of Hong Kong residents had come to the Garden for an outing, but they were outnumbered by camera-bearing tourists, the majority of them German and Japanese, with the latter always traveling in large, compact groups. Douglas noted, in spite of his preoccupation, that there were few Americans on hand.

He walked to the inner end of the Garden, where an eight-story pagoda tower stood alone in the rocky foothills. Paying scant attention to the statues displayed at each level, he climbed to the top floor, then went outdoors to the empty balcony. Eleanor had brought him here on one of their first excursions together, and they had returned many times to enjoy one of the Colony's more spectacular views.

Spread out before him was the crescent of Repulse Bay, one of

Hong Kong's more exclusive resort areas, and riding at anchor in its still waters were some of the world's largest and most luxurious private yachts, the property of local shipping magnates and manufacturers. Farther down the beach was the tiny cove to which Douglas had gone so often with Eleanor on their picnics, and as he gazed at it an unexpected feeling of nostalgia rose up in him. Their relationship, until its bitter ending, had been well worth all of the emotion he had poured into it.

"Waiting for someone, Doctor?"

At the sound of the half-forgotten voice Douglas turned to find Eleanor at his elbow. His first thought was that her eyes were still magnetic. Then he noted that her hair was cut very short, almost like a boy's, and emphasized her huge earrings. She was still in her twenties and, as nearly as he could determine, had not aged a day. Certainly her figure, snug in a minidress of pink silk, was unchanged—and superb.

He hesitated, momentarily at a loss for words, and Eleanor kissed him lightly. "I hope you'll forgive me for tricking you with that cable," she said. "But I couldn't tell you the truth, and I didn't know how else to persuade you to come here."

"Well, I'm here," he said, and his voice was harsher than he knew.

Eleanor ignored the rebuff. "How do I look?"

He saw no reason to avoid paying her the compliment she sought. "Sensational. As always. And as you damn well know."

There was a hint of amusement in her liquid eyes, but it faded as she reached up to touch his hair. "You're growing gray. But I like it. You look distinguished."

If she was trying to soften him she was wasting her time. "Why did you send for me?"

A party of heavy-set Germans emerged onto the balcony, and elbowing their way to the railing, immediately began snapping pictures.

Eleanor's smile was apologetic. "I must speak to you in private. Will you come with me?" Not waiting for a reply, she moved into the pagoda.

Douglas followed, and as they started down the steep, winding stairs she took his arm. The gesture appeared natural, and for a moment the years rolled away, but he continued to suspect she was indulging in deliberate physical gestures. Whatever her motive, he would prove that his armor had thickened.

She didn't speak until they reached the ground level. "My car is parked just outside the side entrance."

He walked beside her, hoping his silence would force her to set the conversational pattern.

They left the grounds, and Eleanor opened the door of a new Jaguar convertible.

Douglas slid across the tooled leather of the passenger's seat, and noted that the car had been driven only a few thousand miles. Whatever her problems might be, she wasn't starving.

She saw him admiring the car. "This was a foolish extravagance," she said, heading in the direction of the heavily populated Central District, where the major hotels and office buildings were located. "There's so much traffic on the roads these days that even in the New Territories I can't drive at full speed."

"At least you can afford a car like this." He ran a hand across a satin-finished walnut panel.

Eleanor hadn't lost the knack of shrugging daintily. "I was one of the few who made money the last time our stock market turned upside down. Perhaps you read about the mania for gambling on the market that struck Hong Kong. Even chambermaids and waiters were investing, and most of them lost their life savings."

"Yes, our newspapers were full of the story." It irritated him to be chatting impersonally with her.

Always quick to gauge his moods, she sensed his hostility. "You just arrived today?"

"This morning, and made an idiot of myself at the hospital."

"It took me a long time to think of a safe and effective way to get in touch with you. I'm sure you'll forgive me when you hear my story."

"That," Douglas said, "appears to be the reason I've just flown ten thousand miles."

Eleanor pulled into the entrance of an apartment building only a few blocks from Douglas' hotel. Leaving the car with the doorman and asking him to park it in the underground garage, she led the way to an elevator. She used three different keys to unlock her front door, Douglas saw, and was careful to bolt and chain the closed door behind them.

They descended three steps from a spacious foyer into a large living room with floor-to-ceiling glass doors that opened onto a terrace overlooking the harbor. To the left was a dining area and kitchen, and through an open door on the right the American caught a glimpse of an oversized bedroom. The place was simply but expensively furnished in an effective blend of traditional Chinese and functional modern, and again it occurred to Douglas that Eleanor was not suffering from a lack of funds. Certainly she was paying far more for this apartment than she had for the flat in which she had lived six years earlier.

"Would you like tea, or may I offer you something stronger?"

He realized she intended to reveal her story only in her own good time, and he reminded himself he was in no hurry. He was here in response to her call, so he tried to curb his impatience. "Whatever you're having will be fine."

Eleanor disappeared into the kitchen, and he heard pots and pans rattle.

Looking around the living room, he was surprised to see his own framed photograph on a table. Unable to judge the significance of its presence, he allowed his gaze to wander, and recognized only her favorite carved jade slab. Everything else in the room appeared to be relatively new.

When Eleanor returned with the tea tray he saw she had freshened her lipstick.

She remembered he liked one lump of sugar and a thin slice of lemon in his tea.

Even though his guard was raised, he felt flattered.

"I hope," she said, "you don't mind seeing your photo. I use my married name, and your picture is proof that I really did have a husband."

Douglas' smile was tight. "Glad to oblige."

Eleanor sat opposite him, a coffee table between them, and offered him a bowl of iced litchi nuts.

He could not resist his favorite Oriental fruit, and peeled a nut, popping the sweet white meat into his mouth.

"I'm surprised," she said, "that in all this time you've never filed suit for divorce."

"I've been so busy building a practice I've never gotten around to it." Douglas knew the explanation sounded lame. "I'd have done something, I'm sure, if I'd found someone else I wanted to marry."

"Then we're still married?"

He couldn't read her expression. "Very much so. I just hope you haven't brought me all the way out here because *you* want a divorce. You could have had it by dropping me a note. And if you want to be the one who files the suit, go ahead. I don't care which of us takes the initiative."

Eleanor ran a slender hand through her tousled hair. "There is nothing on earth I want less, at present, than a divorce from you," she said.

The unexpected response stunned him.

"I've been praying that we still have a valid marriage, Doug. It's what I need, along with your help."

He sipped his tea, making no commitment.

"I know I have no right to ask for anything, and I won't blame you if you turn me down. All I want you to do right now is to hear me out."

No one in the States could make as delicately aromatic a tea.

"I'm not sure where to begin." Managing to look helpless, she took a long, thin cigarette from a box.

He leaned forward to light it for her, his cynical grin indicating his conviction that she had planned her approach with great care.

"For a long time after you went back to America," she said, "I saw very few people. I was in hibernation, hoping you'd change your mind and come back here."

"I told you I wouldn't, any more than you'd change *your* mind and join me in New York."

"I'm not blaming you," Eleanor said, her sincerity genuine. "And I didn't reach out to you this week just to rehash the past and open old wounds. I'm trying to tell you what has happened to me, that's all, and how I came to be in such a mess."

Douglas lighted one of his own cigarettes.

"After a time I did start to go out again, of course, and eventually I drifted into an affair."

He felt his insides tighten, but told himself it was absurd to have expected that she would remain abstinent for all these years.

"The affair has gone on for a long time now—"

"I don't mean to pry," Douglas interrupted, "but if I'm to understand I've got to ask questions as they occur to me. I assume your friend has been keeping you?"

"Never!" Her porcelain façade shattered, and she became intense. "I've supported myself, as I always have, except for the short time you insisted I accept your U. S. Army checks."

He nodded, but made no comment.

"The relationship has grown worse and worse," Eleanor said, "and about three months ago it became so unbearable I ended the affair. Except it isn't ended as far as he's concerned. He's a strange man, Doug. He's violently jealous, and he made dreadful scenes if I as much as spoke to someone else at a party. I knew he meant it when he finally threatened to kill me. That's when I broke away from him. I moved here without even telling him my new address, and I have an unlisted telephone."

"Who is this guy?"

"He's a Scotsman, his name is Ian MacLeod, and he's in the import-export business. He has offices here and in London, and he spends about half his time here every year. He's been in London lately, but he's due to arrive in Hong Kong soon, and I'm frightened."

His manner became professional. "A great many jealous people are emotionally disturbed and are inclined to talk wildly at times. But most of them are harmless."

Eleanor folded her hands in her lap, and spoke in a matter-of-fact voice. "When Ian returns from London in the next few days he'll kill me."

"You can't be serious," Douglas said.

"I am, and you're my only protection. He knows you're my husband, so he won't interfere if you'll take me to Taiwan or Japan. I won't be a burden to you. Just travel with me—as my legal husband—to Tokyo, and stay there a short time with me. Then I'll disappear, and I'll stay hidden until Ian cools off."

He still found it difficult to accept what she was saying at face value. "Sure you don't want to come back to New York with me?"

"I'd even go there, if you insisted. But I don't want to embarrass you, Doug. And you'd have too many impossible explanations to offer people if you showed up with a wife—who vanished after a short time."

Douglas held out his cup for more tea. "Sorry to be skeptical, Eleanor, but what makes you so positive this MacLeod will choke you to death, or whatever?"

"He'll do it with a Lilliput if he's merely cold-blooded, and he'll use a .357 Magnum if he's in one of his vicious moods. I know he'll do it because I won't be the first."

Douglas raised an eyebrow. "You mean he's murdered other mistresses because he has an uncontrollable jealous streak?"

"I'm being serious, I assure you. He's had business associates who have tried to trick him or cheat him, and he's made sure they'll never do it again. Ian is a violent, dangerous man who can't tolerate being crossed. By anyone."

He saw she meant what she was saying, and his smile faded. "Are you trying to tell me he's a gangster or crook of some sort?"

"MacLeod Limited is a highly respected and respectable company, both here and in London. I've made several trips to England with him, and I know how much people there think of him."

"If you're really in danger," Douglas said, "I suggest you go to the police."

"I can't!" Eleanor was alarmed.

"Damned if I can see why not. If your life has been threatened, and you take the threat seriously—"

"The police wouldn't believe me. And even if they did they couldn't protect me from Ian. When he wants vengeance he lets nothing stand in his way. You're the only one who can help me, Doug. That's why I swallowed my pride after all these years and came to you. It wasn't easy, but I had to do it."

"If you won't get in touch with the police I will," Douglas said.

"No! I forbid it!" Her voice rose to a shout, and she jumped to her feet, her fists clenched.

At least she wasn't play-acting, he thought; her fear was real, and he couldn't help sympathizing with her. "I don't know I'd be of any help by escorting you to Tokyo or Taipei," he said, "and I don't see why you'd need me for the purpose. Why couldn't you go off to Japan by yourself?"

"Because Ian and some of his people would realize I was running away and would try to stop me. I've spent a long time trying to work this out, and the only way I can leave here safely is by going with you."

If she wasn't exaggerating, Douglas thought, it was imperative that the police be notified. Rather than risk an even more hysterical reaction, however, he would handle the matter himself, in his own way. "Give me a little time to absorb all this," he said. "I suggest you meet me for dinner tonight, and we can discuss the next step."

VI

The office of Chief Inspector Li of the Hong Kong police reflected the personality of the man. The whitewashed walls were bare, as was the hardwood floor; the Out basket on his desk was overflowing, but no papers littered any other portion of the desk. Li was a short, muscular man who wore a brightly colored sports shirt and, for the sake of his own comfort, had opened his windows wide and turned off his air conditioner. The room was stifling, but he appeared impervious to the heat.

Occasionally he scribbled a few words on a pad as he listened to Douglas' recital, and twice he interrupted his visitor's monologue to issue instructions on the telephone in a soft voice. But he made no direct comment until the American had finished. Then he smiled without humor.

"Your story is bizarre, Doctor," he said, "but we're accustomed to the unusual. Hong Kong is one of the world's crossroads, so we get all kinds here, and I no longer regard any case as strange."

"What I want to know," Douglas replied, "is whether there's any basis for Mrs. Gordon's fears. Until today I hadn't seen her in six years, you understand, so I have no way of gauging whether her alleged dangers are real or whether she's suffering from a form of suppressed neurotic hysteria. I suspect the threats may be a paranoid manifestation, although I'd want a corroborating diagnosis from a psychiatrist before I'd go quite that far. Her refusal to come to you seems to indicate the same symptoms, too."

The Chief Inspector shook his head. "Not necessarily, Doctor. Mrs. Gordon's refusal to deal with the police is something I can understand all too well, I'm afraid. A great many of our citizens feel as she does."

"It's been my impression that you have an exceptionally efficient force."

"We do, but we're still victims of what we call the Asian syndrome. We use many methods to avoid corruption, but some of our officers have known desperate poverty in their time, so they're susceptible to bribery. Our record is good, and only a handful of officers have given in to temptation. But whenever the newspapers uncover a case—and it may happen once or twice a year—the public loses confidence in the entire force. It's one of our burdens, and I'm speaking to you frankly because you'll find thousands here, people of every class, who share Mrs. Gordon's lack of faith in us."

A tap sounded at the door, and a young detective who wore a pistol in a shoulder holster came in and deposited a single sheet of paper on his superior's desk.

Li read it with care, then turned back to his visitor. "Ian MacLeod has no criminal record, Doctor. He paid a fine for speeding on the Kowloon Overpass last year, but that's been his only brush with us. Our industrial and business investigations division finds nothing in its files to indicate that MacLeod Limited is anything other than a firm that sells Hong Kong chinaware, television sets and minicomputers to wholesalers in Great Britain. So, as nearly as we can judge, MacLeod is a legitimate trader."

"There's nothing to back up Mrs. Gordon's claim that people who have opposed him have been murdered?"

"Nothing." Li spread his hands and smiled. "Which isn't to say these supposed murders haven't taken place. We're like the police of any other overcrowded metropolitan society, and there are many crimes that have never been called to our attention."

"I see." Douglas became increasingly convinced that Eleanor was the victim of her own imagination.

"You'll also be relieved to hear that I ordered a check made on Mrs. Gordon while we were about it, and we have no file on her under either the Gordon or Chang names."

"That's good to hear. I've never known the source of her income, and I've wondered."

"To be blunt," the Chief Inspector said, "we'd know it if she were a call girl. She isn't."

"Thank you, and forgive me for wasting your time, Inspector." Douglas stood.

"Not at all. That's why we're here, Doctor. I hope you won't think a personal observation impertinent. It may be that Mrs. Gordon has been regretting her refusal to join you in America, so she's invented a rather colorful story in the hope of winning your sympathy and persuading you to take her to the States."

"The same thought has occurred to me."

Li escorted the visitor to the elevator at the end of the corridor. "In all fairness to the lady, you may want to make a further check before you draw any final conclusions."

"How do I do that?"

"The police are concerned only with the maintenance of order on a local scale. The Preventive Service deals with industrial smuggling, drugs and the like. They keep separate records, so there's an outside chance you might find something in their files."

Having drawn one blank, Douglas didn't seek another, and he hoped that tonight he would be able to persuade Eleanor to admit she had been tricking him.

The restaurants of Hong Kong catered to every palate, and menus ranging from Chinese of every variety to French, Italian, the Deep South of the United States and kosher were available to those who sought variety. Only a few combined the best of national and ethnic tastes in an international mélange, and of these none was more glittering than the dining room located on the top floor of a new Kowloon skyscraper hotel. A wide variety of dishes tempted local industrialists and English executives, semi-official delegations from Red China and American businessmen.

The clientele proved the falsehood of the assertion that the ladies of Hong Kong were dowdy. Chinese in *cheongsams,* Indians in *saris* and women of a score of nationalities in Western cocktail dresses were prominent in forming an assemblage that could be duplicated nowhere else on earth.

The view added to the glamour of the place, too. The restaurant rotated slowly, and without leaving his chair the visitor could see the lights of Hong Kong Island across the harbor, then gaze out at the dark green hills of China in the distance.

But Douglas had no interest in the food, the view or other diners. He concentrated his full attention on the elegantly clad young woman who had lived with him as his wife for a brief time and who still bore his name. Her beauty was an ever-present reminder of the love he had felt for her in the past, and her stubborn refusal to change the story she had told him was an irritation that was gradually causing him to lose his self-control.

"The police records don't lie," he said.

Eleanor continued to eat her filet and salad. "Neither do I."

"I wouldn't call your cablegram the truth!"

"That," she replied with a maddening logic of her own, "was a necessity. But I held back nothing this afternoon."

"If what you really want is to go to New York with me and try to work out a marriage, just say so. Then we'll both know where we stand, and we can make an honest examination of the situation."

She shook her head, and her long earrings jangled. "I've always felt it would be wrong for me to live in America. It would be so easy to agree, to go with you, but both of us would regret it."

Douglas had no intention of repeating the arguments that had ended in their breakup six years earlier, but her stand confused him. Apparently he was mistaken, as was Inspector Li, in believing she had sent for him in an attempt to revive their marriage and accompany him to New York.

Eleanor saw his expression and smiled. "You think I'm stubborn, but you're worse. I've told you why I need your help, but you won't accept my reasons."

"You told me MacLeod is a murderer, but the police know nothing about him."

"He's far too clever," she said.

Douglas summoned the waiter and ordered coffee and brandy. He was convinced she had made up the story she had told him, but it served no useful purpose to insist she was a liar. By escorting her to Tokyo he would risk becoming involved with her again, which wouldn't be difficult, and he had no intention of taking the chance. His increased work schedule would be overwhelming when he returned home, so he'd be wise to leave without delay.

Eleanor sensed that he was backing away and knew him too well to press. Instead she dropped the subject and began to question him about his life as a surgeon.

"Well," he said, "I've achieved most of my goals. I've built a solid practice that's still growing, and a number of prominent physicians refer their surgical cases to me. I can't ask for more than that."

"Are you happy?"

He replied with care. "I'm pleased that I've done exactly what I hoped to do."

"I mean your personal life, not your profession. You've never wanted to marry someone else?"

"Not yet. I haven't had time."

"Then your life has been empty."

"I haven't been celibate all these years."

"But there is no woman who interests you," she persisted.

He thought of Eve Harrell. "Not until recently."

"I knew there was someone." Eleanor sounded smug. "I'm relieved for you. Some men are meant to live as bachelors, but you aren't the type. You're as domestic as I am."

"Which isn't saying much, judging by your record."

She ran a hand through her hair in a gesture he recognized as characteristic. "I thought I'd settle down with Ian, but I was mistaken. I couldn't spend my life with a man that jealous."

"You haven't found anyone else?"

"No, and I'm not looking. All I want is to get out of my present trouble."

She was consistent, he thought, even if her story didn't quite hang together.

"May I be frank with you, Doug? I've miscalculated in one way."

He thought he knew what she meant, and braced himself.

"I believed everything was dead between us. But it isn't. The spark—the magnetic action—whatever it is that draws two people together—is still there for you and me."

He had realized it when they met on the pagoda balcony that afternoon, but he was reluctant to make matters still more complicated by admitting he felt much as she did. "I'm not sure the spark ever dies after a man and woman have felt a mutual attraction," he said. "The danger is that what they recognize is only the illusion of a spark. Perhaps the afterglow."

"Whatever it is," she said, "I find it oddly exciting."

He did, too, and wished she were less candid.

"I hadn't thought of you in that way," Eleanor continued. "All I knew was that you were the only one who could help me. But here we are. And still married, too."

"A legal formality," Douglas said, struggling hard against the tide.

"Or a bond that has never been dissolved."

Certainly she was making herself available, regardless of whether she was acting deliberately or unconsciously.

Aware that he was exercising restraint, Eleanor placed her hand on his for a moment, then withdrew it. "I'm not fooling myself, Doug. I realize it was my fault things didn't work out for us, and I'm still unable to meet your terms. So I know you owe me nothing."

Douglas decided to speak with equal candor. "If we slept together," he said, "it would be far more difficult for me to turn down your request. I'd be obligated to travel to Tokyo with you."

"I still wouldn't be able to make any demands on you. If I'm not going to have any tomorrows, then I want every possible pleasure today."

She wasn't giving up, and he told himself to beware. No matter what her obscure motives might be, she wasn't above using her considerable sex appeal to achieve her ends. The restaurant air conditioning chilled him, and he felt a sudden desire for fresh air.

Summoning their waiter, he paid the check.

Eleanor took his arm as they made their way to the exit, and he realized others were watching them. No matter how complex and unfathomable her nature, her beauty created an aura that inevitably attracted the attention of everyone who saw her.

She could be his again, but only on a temporary basis, and he was uncertain whether the joys of the moment would be worth the pain that would follow. He had needed a long time to recover his equilibrium when he left her in Hong Kong six years ago, and didn't want to repeat the experience. While it was true they were married, a resumption of intimacy would be more like a brief affair, and he hoped he would have the will power to refrain.

There were others in the elevator, so they did not speak on the ride to the ground floor. Eleanor took his arm again as they walked to the rear of the lobby and emerged into the open at the entrance to the hotel parking lot.

The heat struck Douglas like a physical blow, and he halted. He had forgotten that the temperature rarely fell more than a few degrees after sundown in Hong Kong, and the furnacelike humidity drained him of energy. He couldn't remember feeling the heat so intensely on his earlier visits to the Colony, and reflected that his reaction now was a sure sign he was growing older.

Only a few cars were parked in the lot, most of the commuters who rented space having gone home for the night, and the couple sauntered toward Eleanor's Jaguar. Memories continued to flood Douglas, and feeling an inevitability about what was ahead, he became more tense. No matter how great his resolve, it would be virtually impossible to avoid making love to her.

Suddenly Eleanor screamed and pointed.

Directly ahead, bearing down on them at breakneck speed, was a heavy sedan, its headlights extinguished. There was no time to think, and Douglas reacted instinctively by pushing the girl violently out of the path of the onrushing automobile. At the last possible instant he leaped aside, too, and sprawled on the tarred surface, the car barely grazing him as it shot past.

As Douglas hauled himself to his feet the car turned, its tires screeching in protest, and came toward him again. There was no place he could hide, and he knew it was useless to run. He could discern the outlines of two men in the darkened front seat, but could not see their faces clearly enough to identify them, or even determine whether they were Chinese or Caucasian.

Escape was impossible, and the one thought that went through his mind was that he would die without knowing why he was being killed.

Suddenly a sharp, cracking noise sounded above the whine of the engine and a hole appeared in the windshield, surrounded by spreading veins of cracked glass.

The vehicle swerved, missing Douglas by no more than a foot or two, and roared out of the lot into Kowloon traffic.

Stunned by the experience, his mind still unable to function, Douglas turned and saw Eleanor behind him, her dress torn and a dirt-smeared bruise on one shoulder. In her right hand she held a tiny Lilliput pistol to which a silencer was attached, and the weapon was still smoking.

Her smile was tight as Douglas ran to her side. "They were after you as well as me," she said. "Now you may believe my danger is real."

VII

Rarely publicized and virtually unknown to laymen anywhere, the Hong Kong Preventive Service was a law enforcement and investigative agency unlike any other single body in the world. Its one thousand employees performed a variety of duties, including supervision of customs and the prevention and detection of the smuggling of drugs, precious gems, gold and industrial alcohol. Its officers and enlisted men manned border outposts and points of entry, and its weapons included helicopters, aircraft and a fleet of cutters that patrolled the great harbor and dozens of outer islands.

The organization's headquarters, incongruously located in offices on the top floors of a parking garage, housed some of the most sophisticated wireless sending and receiving equipment on earth. Unseen sentries studied every visitor through hidden vents, and every outsider was photographed by automatic cameras. Uniformed officials from every branch of the Service, including the personnel from its own training academy, hurried up and down the silent corridors, their very bearing indicating that they were men and women who belonged to an elite unit in which they took pride.

The nominal chief of the Service was a member of the Governor's cabinet, but the actual director was the Deputy Commissioner, whose uniform shoulder boards indicated that he held a rank equivalent to that of a brigadier. Sir Frederick Simpson was a type seen only in a few places since the decline of the British Empire. The Preventive Service had been his life for more than thirty years, but he was still patient and soft-spoken, the frustrations he had encountered having had no visible effect on him. His gray hair was clipped short, he wore his khaki with easy grace and he courteously insisted on offering his visitor midmorning tea before they began their conversation.

A Chinese secretary observed the amenities as she served the tea in the comfortable, somewhat threadbare inner sanctum, fostering the illusion that no one worked very hard here and that time was unimportant. Sir Frederick sipped his tea, filled a pipe with slow deliberation and looked out of a window at the scores of ships, junks and sampans constantly on the move in the harbor.

"Your Consul General rang me up, Doctor, to tell me you're a person of some prominence in your profession and urging me to extend you my cooperation. Consider it extended." His smile was encouraging.

Douglas stubbed out his cigarette, lighted another and told his story, omitting no essential detail.

The Deputy Commissioner interrupted just once. "So Inspector Li told you the police have no file on Ian MacLeod, did he? That was to be expected."

Douglas didn't know what to make of the comment, but went on with his recital, concluding with an account of the incident in the Kowloon hotel parking lot.

Sir Frederick continued to gaze out at the harbor. "What make of car was it, Doctor?"

Douglas was chagrined. "I was too startled to notice. But it was bigger than most of the cars here, so I'd say it was probably of American manufacture."

"Could you recognize the driver and his companion if I showed you some photographs?"

The American shook his head. "Everything happened so fast that I barely realized there were two men in the car."

The Deputy Commissioner showed no disappointment. "It's fortunate that Mrs. Gordon is a sharpshooter."

"Is she?"

"I'd certainly say so, although I've never met the lady. You tell me she described her pistol as a Lilliput."

"Yes, sir."

"Very difficult to handle, and doubly hard to strike a target when it has been equipped with a silencer."

"I imagine desperation improved her aim," Douglas said. "I doubt very much that she's an expert. She was trembling so hard she couldn't drive, and was still so upset after we reached her flat that I had to administer a sedative."

"Anyone who comes within Ian MacLeod's orbit has good cause to be disturbed," Sir Frederick said.

Douglas felt as though a pitcher of ice water had been poured down his back. "You know him!"

"Good heavens, yes! As MacLeod himself would be the first to tell you, some of my best undercover agents have been building a dossier on him for years. I daresay I'm better acquainted with every detail of his life than I am with the backgrounds of my own wife and children. Not that he cares. We belong to some of the same clubs, and when he's in Hong Kong he goes out of his way to speak to me."

"I'm afraid I don't understand, Sir Frederick."

"Simple, really. MacLeod is a slippery devil, and we've never been able to gather enough hard evidence to bring charges against him. The man has a genius for escaping from every trap we've set for him. I know he laughs at me, but there's been nothing I've been able to do about it. Yet." The Deputy Commissioner continued to look unperturbed.

"His company is crooked?"

"Not at all. MacLeod Limited is a legitimate business enterprise. We've looked into every phase of his operations, and so has Scotland Yard. His business is clean, even though it's only a front for his smuggling."

Douglas leaned forward, his tea forgotten. "Drugs, I suppose."

"Nothing that nasty. MacLeod is a gentleman engaged in the most civilized of criminal pursuits. What do you know about gold, Doctor?"

"Very little," Douglas said. "I read a magazine piece not long ago to the effect that the peasants of India and Indonesia will pay almost any black market price for gold, which not only represents security to them, but assumes an almost mythological significance. I was interested because the same was true of the poor people in Vietnam when I was stationed there some years ago. But that's the extent of my knowledge."

"A few plain facts will fill you in. Three syndicates, all European-owned, control the better part of the world's illegal drug trade. The Chiu Chow of northern Thailand and Burma—Chinese warlords who have established their own opium poppy kingdom in the Golden Triangle—are partners in one, which is the roughest of the lot."

"MacLeod is in business with them?"

Sir Frederick was amused. "Hardly. He uses violence only as a last resort. He's on the second level of management, one of the operating directors, of a syndicate in which several wealthy men in London have a part interest."

Douglas was sickened by the thought that Eleanor had been the mistress of a prominent gold smuggler, but he tried to absorb what the Deputy Commissioner was telling him.

"Most of the gold is mined in South Africa, although some comes from Turkey and other places. The portion diverted to the black market, which can be a considerable amount, goes openly to Dubai, the Arab oil sheikdom that has the only deep-sea port on the Persian Gulf. Quantities of it are then sent here, part by air, but most of it smuggled in by sea." Sir Frederick went to the window and beckoned.

Douglas joined him, and looked down at the harbor.

"Thousands of vessels come in and go out every month. Technically Hong Kong is a free port, so the Preventive Service is interested principally in halting the smuggling of certain items, gold among them. But we lack the manpower to search every ship, and I estimate we seize no more than fifteen percent of the illegal gold."

"The rest slips into the mainstream of legitimate gold?"

The Deputy Commissioner shook his head. "You underestimate the smugglers. They sneak it over to Macao, the Portuguese colony located a short distance from here, which has no restrictions on the import or export of precious metals. The bullion goes to the smelters of a private bank, where experts convert it into little one-kilo bars, jewelry, medallions, thin flakes the size of your thumbnail—as many shapes as you can imagine. Then it comes back through Hong Kong for distribution to the peasants of the East, who will pay two to three times the legitimate market price. Recently in the Philippines some villagers paid quadruple the official price."

"If you know so much about the smugglers, why don't you put them out of business, Sir Frederick?"

"Because the only people we catch are the couriers, the actual carriers, who are small fry. Most of them know nothing whatever about their superiors and couldn't identify them. I doubt if even the Portuguese bankers in Macao, or the officials of Red China who allow the trade to flourish because their government takes a share of the profits, know anyone but the couriers. The top-level smugglers have a genius for self-protection."

"Eleanor must have learned something about MacLeod's operations during the years she lived with him. Suppose she could be persuaded to go into court and testify—"

"You've been misled, Doctor," the Deputy Commissioner said. "MacLeod has been married for more than ten years to a charming, vivacious—and shrewd—lady, who goes everywhere with him. Mrs. Gordon isn't his mistress now, and has never been his mistress."

Eleanor had some errands to do in Kowloon, she told Douglas when he telephoned her, and explaining that she thought it a sensible precaution to make different meeting arrangements, she set a time and place.

His attempts to curb his impatience were only partly successful, and his temper began to rise as he took the Star Ferry across the harbor. In the past he had enjoyed the quarter of an hour ride, but now he could think only of Eleanor's double-dealing. She had brought him to Hong Kong on a ruse, and she had lied to him when presumably telling him the truth. At the same time, however, the attempt to murder both of them in the hotel parking lot last night had been both real and frightening, and he intended to get to the bottom of the situation.

Disembarking on Kowloon side, Douglas walked the short distance to the head of Nathan Road. Ahead stretched the Golden Mile, which boasted some of the world's finest jewelry and fur stores, boutiques, antique shops and other retail establishments, most of them posting prices only a fraction of what was charged elsewhere. He had only a short time to wait.

Eleanor approached him, dressed for the first time since his return in a brocaded *cheongsam*. Her eyes came alive when she saw him, and she greeted him with a warm, lingering kiss, as though she had no cares. "You were kind to me last night when I was so jittery," she said, "and I won't forget it." Taking his arm, she started down the Golden Mile. "I thought we could window-shop, and when we're hungry we can stop in somewhere for a drink and a sandwich."

Douglas realized she had converted a confrontation into a social occasion, but it was impossible to discuss important matters on a public street, so he was forced to fall in with her way of doing things.

"You sounded so grim when you called me this morning," she said. "I hope your mood has improved."

"My mood," he said, "will depend on you."

"How flattering." She squeezed his arm.

It was pointless to explain that he wasn't paying her a compliment. But he was beginning to see what he hadn't realized when he had married her, that she had a real talent for manipulating others.

Eleanor paused in front of a large jewelry store, studied the display in a plate glass window and pointed to a pair of dangling gold earrings. "Those will go perfectly with this dress. Let's look at them." Giving him no chance to reply, she entered the store.

As Douglas followed her he wondered whether she was planning to use him financially, as she seemed to be doing in other ways. Ever since the two-year period when she had received a substantial portion of his Army pay he had wondered whether she had been greedy, trapping him while the bonanza had lasted.

She tried on the earrings and turned to him for his approval.

"Very nice," he said, trying not to sound too enthusiastic but admitting to himself that her taste was faultless.

"I'll take them," she told the sales clerk. "In fact, I'll wear them."

The price was one hundred and fifty dollars in Hong Kong money, or about thirty American dollars, and Douglas reached into his pocket for his wallet.

Eleanor caught his wrist. "No," she said, "I won't allow you to pay for them. I wouldn't have bought them if I'd thought you would."

He was surprised, and hastily revised his estimate of her. Yet he couldn't help wondering whether her insistence on paying for the earrings herself had been a deliberate gesture intended to lull any suspicions he might be developing. He shook his head in a vain attempt to clear it, telling himself he was becoming so enmeshed in Oriental subtlety that he was destroying his own ability to think clearly.

Again she paused, this time to admire a black mink coat. "One of the chief reasons I'm sorry I didn't go to the States with you, Doug, is because I've always wanted a mink. But I have no need for one here, and I won't be in Tokyo long enough to use one there. I'll have left Japan far behind before the cold weather arrives."

It would do no harm to pry. "Mink, particularly this quality, is expensive."

"Very," she said.

He raised an eyebrow, allowing his unasked question to hang in the air.

"I may have a great many worries," she said, "but they aren't financial."

"That's good to know." It occurred to him that he could maneuver her into a corner. "Apparently MacLeod is generous."

She side-stepped so deftly that he wondered if she could read his mind. "I have no need for Ian's money. I wouldn't care in the least if he never gave me a penny."

Douglas was stymied, short of demanding to know the source of her income, and it was premature to take that blunt an approach.

Eleanor continued to window-shop with enthusiasm for the better part of an hour, but suddenly looked stricken. "This can't be much fun for you, Doug. You must be starved."

She took him to a tiny exclusive restaurant across the street, where the drinks were generous and there was an almost endless variety of *dim sun,* or appetizer-like dishes, all of them bite-sized and most cooked in dumplings or pastry.

Douglas waited until they had ordered a second drink before he opened the subject that was so much on his mind. "I've been wondering whether MacLeod was behind the wheel of that car last night."

"Impossible!"

"But you told me that when he becomes jealous he's capable of committing any act of violence." He felt sure he was tightening the noose.

"He does go wild," she said. "But he couldn't have been driving the car. He's still in England."

"Maybe he flew back here without your knowledge."

"When Ian returns," Eleanor said, "I'll know it. I'll be notified thirty minutes after his airplane lands."

"You're very sure of yourself."

"In some things."

"Then you must have a pretty good idea who those men were last night."

She shook her head, averting her gaze.

"Men MacLeod hired to do his dirty work for him."

"He wouldn't do it that way, not when he's dealing with me."

"And why did they want to kill me? Just yesterday you assured me that MacLeod knows you and I are married, and wouldn't interfere if I took you to Tokyo or Taipei."

"He wouldn't." She was defensive now, but remained calm.

"Well, somebody objected rather strenuously, and all I did was to take you to dinner."

"I haven't sorted it out yet, but I will. I was going to suggest that we leave for Japan at once, later today. But it might be wiser—and safer—to wait a few days."

"What's to be gained?" Douglas persisted. "They did their damnedest to kill us, and they may try again."

"Not if we take precautions. It isn't easy to make a double murder look accidental."

"Long before I went to medical school," he said, "I learned the shortest distance between two points is a straight line. A line that starts in Hong Kong and goes nonstop to Tokyo. I see no advantage in making ourselves targets in a shooting gallery."

"Before I dropped off to sleep last night," Eleanor said, "I decided I've been trying to take a coward's way out. I want to wait until Ian arrives and have it out with him. Once I've convinced him that my husband is the man who has succeeded him in my life he may be willing to give me up."

Douglas' smile was cold. "I'd like to sit in on that little session."

"It would be embarrassing."

"It wouldn't bother me, and I don't think MacLeod would be upset, either. Because you aren't having an affair with him, and never did."

Her eyes met his without faltering, and to his astonishment, she made no attempt to maintain her deception. It appeared to be enough that he had learned the truth, and she actually smiled as she leaned back in her chair.

"No challenge?" he demanded. "No argument?"

"There's very little I can say." Eleanor looked remarkably self-possessed as she sipped her drink.

"Aren't you even going to ask how I found out?"

She removed one of her long cigarettes from a silver case, tapped it and took her time lighting it. "There are many people in Hong Kong who know Ian MacLeod. Even an amateur detective could pick up basic facts from any of them."

Douglas found it difficult to keep his voice down. "I think I have a right to know why you lied to me again."

"Maybe I was trying to make *you* jealous."

"After all these years of separation? I can't buy that line, Eleanor. Why should you care how I feel toward you—or whether I feel anything at all?"

Her shrug indicated a refusal to quarrel with him. "I'd rather spare you my problems."

He could scarcely believe that she offered him neither an explanation nor an apology.

Her expression bland, Eleanor reached into her alligator shoulder bag and took out several keys affixed to a chain. "I had these made for you today. They're for my apartment, and I think we'd be safer to go there separately. That will make a repetition of last night's unpleasantness less likely. I've instructed the building staff to admit you, and I suggest we meet there at five this afternoon. I must attend to some errands after lunch, and if I should be a little late help yourself to a drink."

VIII

Common sense nagged at Douglas, urging him to leave Hong Kong without delay and return to his waiting practice in New York. But he was intrigued by the mystery of Eleanor's predicament, and her lies acted as goads that involved him more deeply. After traveling almost halfway around the world he thought he should wait until he had learned enough to satisfy his curiosity, and he knew it would bother him to leave with so many questions still unanswered. Besides, he rationalized, he hadn't taken a vacation in a long time and he was enjoying a respite from the operating and examination rooms.

His principal reason for staying was more difficult to admit. He realized anew that Eleanor was as untrustworthy as her conduct was erratic, but she fascinated him and he was drawn to her now, just as he had been when he first knew her. Even harder to admit was that he wanted her. No other woman had ever given him such deep, lasting gratification, and the knowledge that they were still married made the resumption of intimacy even more tempting. Certainly he couldn't put all the blame on her for the complexity of their relationship.

Returning alone to Hong Kong side after lunch, he started to wander in the direction of his hotel, but on sudden impulse he hailed a taxi and ordered the driver to take him to Eleanor's apartment building. It was not yet 4 P.M., and as she had indicated she wouldn't return for at least another hour he would have ample time to snoop. It wasn't illegal for a man to look through his wife's belongings, and although he had no idea what he might find it was possible he might stumble across some clues that would help solve the puzzle that her lies had compounded.

He could always tell himself that he intended to play detective solely for the preservation of his own skin. He had no enemies either here or at home, and he knew no one who hated him enough to seek his death. He could no longer doubt that Eleanor was a murder target, but she had done her best to prevent him from learning the reason. Now that he was on the list, too, the least he could do would be to learn a few solid facts.

The doorman greeted Douglas with a salute and smile, and the major-domo in the lobby bowed him to the self-service elevator. At least Eleanor had been truthful when she told him the building staff was prepared for his arrival.

He fumbled for a short time with the keys, but finally managed to open all of the door locks. Then, remembering the precautions Eleanor had taken, he bolted himself in.

The flat was empty, as she had told him it would be, and he began his search by looking through the contents of her bathroom medicine chest. He saw a variety of shampoos, two shelves were crammed with cosmetics of all kinds, and another was filled with bottles of nail polish. Finally, adjacent to a hair dryer, he found a small bottle of aspirin and a somewhat larger container of Vitamin C tablets. Obviously Eleanor enjoyed radiant health and her problem did not lie in that direction.

The kitchen and living room were neat, and he recalled that he had always admired her orderliness. Feeling slightly ashamed, he went into her bedroom, and in the top drawer of a small cabinet he found the key to a safe-deposit box and a checkbook. She kept an account in the Hong Kong branch of one of London's more prominent banks, and the size of her balance surprised him. She kept more than a hundred thousand dollars in the account, or twenty thousand in American money, a considerable sum. Leafing through the book, he saw she had written checks to the building management for rent, to a market for food and to a liquor store. A number of checks were made out to boutiques, shoe stores and a cosmetics shop, and she had made regular, modest withdrawals for cash. No checks indicated any payments that were out of the ordinary, and she had made no deposits in the two and a half months she had used this book. By the time Douglas put the book back in the drawer he was feeling a trifle foolish.

Dresser drawers were filled with neat piles of sweaters, blouses, lingerie and pantyhose, and he left them untouched. Rows of shoes stood in an old-fashioned French cabinet, and he recalled that footgear had been her greatest extravagance. His search had revealed nothing, and when he came to a huge closet, lined in cedar, he scarcely bothered to glance at the double line of dresses, skirts and robes hanging there. As he was about to close the door again a loose cedar panel at one side of the closet caught his eye, and he noticed a snippet of material behind it.

The panel yielded to his touch, and he pulled out a curious feminine garment, a combination brassiere and belt, the two portions connected by panels, and all of it in nude-colored nylon. Over the years he had seen countless women patients in varying stages of undress, but none of them had ever worn anything quite like it. At both sides of each bra cup he saw small pockets which opened at the top, each about two and one-half inches wide and three and one-half inches high. Eight similar pockets were sewn inside the belt, three in the front, three in the rear and one at each side.

Douglas could not imagine what Eleanor carried in these pockets, and the mere fact that he was in total ignorance gave the garment significance. He discovered that when he folded it carefully it occupied no more space than a handkerchief, and once again giving in to impulse, he thrust it into the inner pocket of his wallet. Pushing the cedar panel back into place, he closed the closet door.

He was too much of a pragmatist to speculate on the meaning of the unknown, and as it was almost 5 P.M. he returned to the kitchen, took some ice from the refrigerator and went to the little bar in the living room. An unopened bottle of Bourbon stood apart from the other bottles, and he was touched. Eleanor had remembered he preferred it to other kinds of whiskey and ordered it that morning from her liquor store. It was difficult to think too harshly of someone that considerate of his welfare.

It was possible the building staff would tell Eleanor when he had arrived, and she would wonder how he had occupied himself, so he gulped down a drink, poured another and then scattered several English and American fashion magazines, the flat's principal reading matter, on the floor beside an easy chair.

Aside from the strange garment he had found nothing of any possible importance in his search. What struck him as odd was the lack of personal touches, other than his silver-framed photograph, in the place. More than neatness had created the sterile effect: it was almost as though Eleanor had moved her clothes into a furnished hotel suite she was occupying for a short time. There were no letters, no mementos, nothing to indicate her habits or any details of her day-to-day living. A police official or a criminal who searched the flat would find literally nothing that would indicate her likes, dislikes or vocation, nothing that would reveal even scraps about her friends, relatives or lovers.

He tried to remember whether her old flat had been this impersonal, but he could recall no details except a bowl of fresh-cut flowers she had kept on a living room table. Come to think of it, there were flowers in a lacquered bowl right now. It was too bad that when he had known her previously he had been too much in love to be conscious of his surroundings.

It was five-fifteen when Eleanor appeared, and unable to open the bolted door, she had to ring the bell. He admitted her to the flat, and she deposited a number of packages on the coffee table.

"I'm afraid I splurged this afternoon," she said. "On a wardrobe for Tokyo." She showed him a cream-colored pantsuit of raw silk, matching pumps and a shoulder bag of almost the same shade. "A half-dozen other things will be sent tomorrow. I'm awful, don't you agree? I'll use any excuse to buy more clothes, and I'm dreadfully extravagant." In spite of her almost childlike excitement she remembered her manners. "You've helped yourself, I see. Good."

"Thank you for the Bourbon. Now I'll return the compliment." He had directed his taxi driver to stop at a liquor store, and he went to the kitchen refrigerator for the bottle of champagne he had bought, and for the chilled wineglass he had placed near it.

Eleanor clasped her hands in delight. "You remembered, too!"

"How could I forget? Years ago you wouldn't drink anything except champagne."

"I still prefer it to everything else." She watched him as he removed the wire cage and began to ease the cork from the bottle.

Douglas glanced in the direction of the bar and raised an eyebrow.

"It's one of my peculiarities. I always keep Scotch on hand for guests, and French brandy. Sometimes *mao tai*," she added, referring to a potent sorghum-based liqueur made only in mainland China. "But I never buy champagne for myself. I drink it only when someone orders it for me."

"Then you should get all you want." He filled the glass and handed it to her. "I'm sure any gentleman who spends an evening with you would be happy to get you a magnum at a time."

"You may not believe this, but I don't lead all that active a social life. I spend most evenings by myself, either going to the theater or watching television. Of course I do travel a bit."

She could have as many suitors as she wanted. "I assume," Douglas said, "your isolation is your own choice."

"I'm afraid I've become something of a loner, as you Americans call it." Suddenly she smiled and raised her glass. "Here's to you and me."

He lifted his own glass in return, then waited a moment before he said, "I doubt if Ian MacLeod has bought you any champagne."

Eleanor looked stricken. "Will you forgive me for telling you such a whopper?"

"Fair enough, if you'll explain a few fundamentals."

She sat gracefully on the divan and sipped her champagne. "I've promised myself I won't lie to you again, Doug, and it's a real promise. But I'll need your cooperation."

He was simultaneously annoyed and amused. "What must I do?"

"Don't ask me any more questions for the present, and I won't feel the need to evade and lie."

"That's a tall order."

"I swear to you," Eleanor said, "that I'll tell you everything. Why I'm in danger, why I sent for you, why it's urgent that I leave Hong Kong for a time. I'll hold nothing back, and you'll not only understand, but you'll realize why I've had to handle all this as I have. I even hope you'll be able to sympathize with me. At the very least you'll realize why I've had to be so secretive and why I've been forced to handle this situation as I have."

Douglas drained his glass, and his tension was so great that he added another splash of Bourbon. Most people regarded him as aggressive, even dominating, but she was one woman he couldn't handle. "When will I hear all these things?"

"Before we leave for Tokyo. Preferably on the evening flight tomorrow. So we'll appear in public as little as possible between now and then."

"Hold on," he said. "You're assuming we're making this trip together. I haven't rejected the idea, but I haven't agreed to escort you anywhere, either."

Eleanor spread her hands in a gesture of finality. "If you refuse," she said in a quiet tone that was far more effective than histrionics, "it will be the end of me. I can do just so much to protect myself, and the longer I stay in Hong Kong the greater the chance becomes that Ian MacLeod will see to it that I'm killed."

He wondered, now that he knew she had never been MacLeod's mistress, why she continued to claim the man was responsible for her plight. "I don't want your death on my conscience, and I have no intention of wandering around empty parking lots late at night, either." He refilled her champagne glass. "There's one thing that mystifies me, and I'm stating a fact, not asking a question."

She watched him over the rim of her glass, her eyes wary.

"You've spent a great many years in Hong Kong. Even though you say you're a loner, there must be close relationships you've developed. Surely there's some friend you can depend on."

There was a hint of sadness in her smile. "I do have one good friend, a man who knew my family in Peking, before Mao Tse-tung seized power in nineteen forty-nine."

This was the first time she had ever admitted what he had guessed, that she was of northern Chinese stock, and might have become a refugee as a child after the collapse of the Nationalist government of Chiang Kai-shek.

"Ho Fang has done more for me than I could possibly tell you," she said. "But he's an elderly illiterate, so there are limits to what he can do, and I'm reluctant to ask too much of him."

Douglas made a mental note of the man's name, hoping that this time she was telling him the truth.

"There are other people I've called friends," Eleanor said. "Both men and women. But I can't count on any of them, not under the circumstances. I learned—long ago—that everyone has a price, and although I don't mind taking reasonable risks I become conservative when my life is at stake."

Her matter-of-fact cynicism was as disturbing as anything he had encountered since his return to Hong Kong. He was unfamiliar with the details of her background, it was true, but it seemed obvious she had led a difficult life that had hardened her and given her such careless disregard for the truth. It was shocking that a lovely young woman who had not yet reached the age of thirty had become so callous, and he told himself to lay aside the personal resentments he had been harboring. At the least she deserved his compassion and, perhaps, whatever humane assistance he could render her.

"There you have it," Eleanor said. "A polar flight to the States leaves in two hours, which gives you enough time to pack your belongings, book a seat and go out to Kaitak Airport. I've done everything I can to enlist your help, and if you want to leave now I won't try to stop you."

Douglas rattled the ice in his glass, but remained seated.

There was a long silence before Eleanor murmured, "May I have a little more champagne, please?"

Again he refilled her glass. She had been sincere in her willingness to allow him to depart without a struggle, and her sudden air of resignation impressed him.

"I should be grateful to you, and I am," she said. "But I'm curious, too, and I hope you'll tell me why."

He tried to order his thoughts, but failed. "I'm not sure," he said at last. "Every doctor feels an urge to help someone who is suffering, but there's more to it than that. Two people can't be happily married, even for a short time, without developing some kind of emotional tie that lasts, or so I'm discovering, and I find my feelings toward you aren't as dead as I thought."

"You've been in and out of my mind a thousand times, too, and I hoped you'd share my reaction. That's why I gambled and sent you the cablegram."

Their eyes met, and Douglas felt incapable of looking away. He was swimming into deep waters, he realized, but a sense of recklessness swept over him and he jumped to his feet.

Eleanor drained her glass, still meeting his gaze, and then she stood, too.

It was impossible for them to articulate their confused thoughts, but at this moment speech was superfluous. They met in front of the divan, lips seeking and bodies straining.

Douglas' last conscious thought was that he felt a sense of *déjà vu*, but a new element had been added to it. Eleanor reacted precisely as he had known she would, her full lips parting for his kiss, one hand gripping the back of his head. Her scent was familiar, and so was every contour of her body. He knew how she would respond to every kiss, and she remembered how to arouse him, too.

At the same time, however, he was aware of an unfamiliar sensation of excitement, an unfulfilled longing for something greater than physical satisfaction. It was a desire he had experienced only once before, when they had made love for the first time, and Eleanor seemed to share his feeling.

The floor rocked beneath their feet, and they had to steady themselves as they drew apart.

Eleanor led the way into her bedroom, and still they did not speak. She closed the blinds, which cut the strong afternoon sun to thin ribbons of light.

Douglas understood her motive. She wasn't being unduly shy, which wasn't her nature, but after all their years of living apart a display of discretion was more seemly. She was a lady, no matter what sort of life she had been leading, and deserved to be treated accordingly.

They undressed, neither dawdling nor hurrying, and with one accord moved to the bed. Their nude bodies pressed close together, and Douglas was overwhelmed by erotic desire, forgetting their separation and its cause, her trickery and lies, even his reminder that she was a lady.

Eleanor's desire became compelling, too. Her long, immaculately groomed fingernails raked his back, and she lost the last of her control.

Their tensions became unbearable, and when he took her they found release together.

For a few moments, or perhaps it was an hour, they rested side by side on the bed, drifting in a half-conscious state, their bodies touching. Time had lost its meaning.

At last they stirred, and Eleanor smiled. "We won't go out for dinner," she said. "We'll eat right here, and I'll show you what a good cook I've become."

Douglas welcomed the suggestion, knowing they would make love again and yet again, that the sense of intimacy they shared would be prolonged. The years fell away, and he was a young medical officer from Vietnam, cherishing every moment of his leave with the girl he loved.

IX

The waiting room at Preventive Service headquarters was crowded with early-morning visitors, and Douglas, who had no appointment, was lucky to find an empty place on a wooden bench. There was no conversation, and the men and women who slouched in their seats stared straight ahead into space. Most were relatives of people who had been arrested by Service personnel in the past twenty-four hours, the majority on drug-smuggling charges, and only here was it possible to obtain permits to see the incarcerated.

Douglas, engrossed in his own thoughts, also was oblivious to the proximity of other visitors. He had spent the night at Eleanor's flat, stopping at his hotel only for a change of linen, and he was euphoric over the drastic change in their relationship. He was uncertain whether he had fallen in love with her anew, whether he had ever stopped loving her or whether he had merely fallen prey to a romantic illusion when he saw her again. It didn't matter. She was the most beautiful and charming of women, and she was still his wife. Basking in the afterglow of their lovemaking, he could even imagine that he might persuade her to make her life in New York with him. His bitterness and frustration had vanished and been replaced by an optimism more buoyant than he had known in years.

At the same time, however, he was so suffused with guilt that he felt a deep depression. He had returned to the Preventive Service offices to obtain Sir Frederick Simpson's opinion of the strange, harnesslike undergarment he had found in Eleanor's apartment, and he couldn't rid himself of the belief that he was being disloyal to her—immediately after sleeping with her.

He was willing to grant that she had lied to him and fooled him, but he had no reason to doubt her promise to tell him her complete story. He couldn't help it, however, that one corner of his mind refused to be taken in. Just as growths had to be cut from a human body with a surgeon's knife to restore sound health, so it was necessary to allay his half-formed suspicions before he could fully enjoy his renewed intimacy with Eleanor. He was here for no purpose other than to rid himself of his doubts.

After he had waited only a short time an officer in the dark blue uniform of the Protective Division naval patrol, a pistol hanging in a holster suspended from his belt, led the American down the long corridor. Teletypes chattered in a large central area, spelling out the latest news from Reuters, the Associated Press, United Press International and Interpol, the international police organization jointly maintained by more than sixty nations. Secretaries were brewing coffee and tea in outer offices, and young messengers were distributing morning newspapers published in both English and Chinese.

Through the open door of a conference room the visitor caught a glimpse of a khaki-clad officer wearing the shoulder boards of a commander, who stood before a map of the outer islands, and a number of the rank and file, seated before him, were scribbling rapidly in notebooks. Somewhere in the distance a loudspeaker was amplifying a conversation between a helicopter unit and a ground crew, and an exceptionally attractive young Eurasian woman, the upper part of her face concealed by a floppy-brimmed hat, came past Douglas from the opposite direction without bothering to glance at him. He wondered whether she might be an undercover agent, but decided she was too conspicuous.

A visit to this place caused a man to think in unaccustomed terms, he told himself, and he was glad he didn't serve on the staff. The Deputy Commissioner and his principal aides spent so much of their lives in the half-world of smuggling, informers and double-dealing that they probably trusted no one.

Sir Frederick was looking through his early mail, and greeted his visitor cordially. "Well, Dr. Gordon, I was wondering whether you'd had enough of the mysterious East and had gone back to the States."

"Not yet," Douglas replied, and apologized for the intrusion as he sat in the chair offered to him. "I may be making a fool of myself, but I did a little amateur detective work yesterday."

Sir Frederick made no comment, but his eyes revealed a quickened interest.

"In Mrs. Gordon's flat. I found an odd contraption hidden there, and thought it might mean more to you than it does to me. I've never seen anything like it." He reached into his wallet, removed the nylon brassiere and belt, and placed the garment on the desk.

The Deputy Commissioner allowed his gaze to rest on it for no more than an instant.

"I found these pockets unusual, and I wondered if you'd know whether they might be used for smuggling of some sort. Packs of cigarettes, maybe—"

"They're the wrong size and shape for cigarette packets," the Deputy Commissioner said, not bothering to examine the brassiere and belt. "Does Eleanor Chang Gordon know you've taken this piece of underwear?"

"To the best of my knowledge, she has no idea, Sir Frederick."

"Come with me to the sanctum sanctorum, why don't you? You'll find the visit instructive." The Deputy Commissioner guided the American into the hall and down a flight of steps.

They made their way through a labyrinth of corridors, coming at last to an area bearing a large sign:

AUTHORIZED PERSONNEL ONLY
By Order of
F. L. C. Simpson
Deputy Commissioner

Turning a corner, Douglas saw a steel mesh gate, guarded by two sentries who carried submachine guns. Both jumped to attention, and Sir Frederick returned their salutes. Then he conducted his guest to a barren room with heavily barred windows. The only item of furniture was a mahogany table, somewhat the worse for wear, on which rested a clothbound notebook.

"We'll sign you in now, Doctor, and fill in your passport number and other vital statistics later."

"I can show you my passport now, Sir Frederick." Douglas reached into the inner pocket of his jacket.

"That won't be necessary. We already have the data on file."

Douglas was startled by the efficiency of the Preventive Service, and saw an amused gleam in the Deputy Commissioner's eyes.

Sir Frederick wrote in the notebook, looking up when two junior officers, both armed with .45 automatics, appeared from another portion of the L-shaped chamber. They saluted, too.

"I've attended to the formalities," their superior told them. "Now I wonder if you'd be good enough to ask Major Yang and Mr. Holcomb to join us."

One of the officers disappeared around the corner, and Douglas could hear a telephone being dialed.

"This section," Sir Frederick told him, "is as secure as modern science can make it. We protect it with fifteen or twenty devices of various kinds, and it is also bomb-proof."

Two senior officials appeared, and were admitted to the room by the sentries after showing their credentials. They were followed by a young lieutenant in a uniform that resembled the dress green and scarlet of the Royal Marines.

Each of them, in turn, went to a steel door that occupied all of one wall and manipulated a separate set of tumbler locks. They were followed by the two junior officers on permanent duty, who did the same. Finally, after all the others had stepped back, Sir Frederick twisted another set of tumblers, then inserted a key into a slot. "It takes six of us to open this door, Doctor, and no one of us knows more than a single combination. I doubt if there's a bank vault on earth this secure."

The heavy metal door opened, and the junior officers drew their guns, the lieutenant doing the same. Anyone who tried to break in now would have a real gun battle on his hands.

Douglas followed the Deputy Commissioner into a room about thirty feet long and approximately half as wide, its two windows protected by double rows of bars and a shield of steel mesh. Its walls were lined with shelves that extended from floor to ceiling, some of them piled with bulky burlap bags that emitted a musklike odor, the others filled with transparent plastic bags of a white powderlike substance.

"This," Sir Frederick said, "is the world's largest collection of confiscated drugs, worth—officially—about five hundred million dollars in your money. The bags contain raw opium, and the glassines are number four heroin, which is cut to one-fourth or one-eighth strength on the black market."

"What do you do with it?"

"We make the bulk of it into morphine that brings the Crown Colony a splendid revenue, and all of it is sold legally, of course. I daresay much of the morphine you've used in your practice was made right here." Sir Frederick walked to a shelf beneath the window and beckoned. "But that isn't why I brought you to the sanctum. Try picking up this little object with your thumb and middle finger."

A surgeon's hands were exceptionally strong, but Douglas found it difficult to do as he had been bidden. A small bar that looked like gold, which was no more than half the thickness of a cigarette pack, was too heavy, and he had to use his other fingers.

"We'll sign that bar out, along with another," Sir Frederick said, and ushered him out of the strange treasure room.

A few minutes later they were back in the Deputy Commissioner's office. Placing the two little bars on the desk, Sir Frederick handed his visitor the brassiere and belt.

"See what you can do with these," he said.

Douglas quickly discovered that each of the bars fitted into any of the pockets perfectly. He was startled, but his mind was clear, and even as he looked inquiringly at his host he thought he knew what he would hear.

"This undergarment," Sir Frederick said, "was custom-made for a female gold-smuggling courier, who took special instruction in learning how to carry twelve bars at any one time. A carrier needs practice in sitting, standing and walking, but the effort is well worth the inconvenience. Depending on the official price, the gold that can be carried at any one time is worth about two hundred and fifty thousand dollars in American money and at least double that on the black market. The experienced courier, who may make six to ten trips into the field each year, earns ten percent of the black market price. A tidy income for someone energetic, and there are no income taxes to be paid. Do you have any questions, Doctor?"

Douglas swallowed hard. "Eleanor—" He stopped short.

"Eleanor Chang Gordon has been high on our list of suspects for a long time. We've felt certain she's acted as a courier for Ian MacLeod's syndicate, but until now we've had no positive proof. Your efforts weren't as amateurish as you thought, and the Preventive Service is in your debt, Dr. Gordon."

"You regard this contraption as positive proof, Sir Frederick?" Douglas' throat was so dry it ached.

"There is no doubt it fits her without a ripple or bulge, as will be demonstrated at the proper time."

"You're placing her under arrest?" Douglas' mind was whirling.

"We're hunting bigger game, and I hope she'll cooperate with us, either willingly or inadvertently. I'm sure the courts would be disposed in her favor." Sir Frederick's Oxonian drawl seemed more pronounced.

"I'm aware of your delicate situation, Doctor, and I don't want to embarrass you. Legally you're the lady's husband, so you can't testify against her. In fact, I have no intention of revealing officially how this garment came into our possession. I'd also like to emphasize that I don't want to burden you with too many confidences."

It was bad enough that Eleanor was a gold smuggler, but Douglas was crushed by the realization that he had played a major role in exposing her. "How long has she been doing this sort of work?"

"She first appears in our records ten years ago, when she was still in her teens."

So she had already been a courier when he first met her on his furlough from the war in Vietnam. He understood, too, why she had no need for money: obviously she had earned a fortune during the past decade.

"You may want to catch the next flight back to New York, Dr. Gordon." The Deputy Commissioner was sympathetic. "I hope I have some idea of what you're feeling, and I can only observe that you've become involved in something beyond your depth."

"So it seems." Douglas made a supreme effort to order his thoughts. "But I can't run off like a disappointed little boy. I've got to see Eleanor again and set the whole record straight with her." He refrained from adding that the situation had become even more complicated, that in the past sixteen hours he and Eleanor had resumed marital relations.

"I thought that's what you'd want to do, Doctor." Sir Frederick leaned forward, placing his elbows on his desk. "I don't want to exert pressure on you, nor do I want to ask you to perform any tasks on behalf of the Protective Service. I want to be fair to you."

"Thanks." When a man in the Deputy Commissioner's position spoke of fairness, it was time to raise one's guard.

"When you've had a chance to sort out this situation in your own mind," Sir Frederick said, "you may decide—of your own free will—that Mrs. Gordon will enjoy the greatest benefits by working directly with us. So you may want to persuade her to drop in for a chat with me. She won't be clapped into irons, and she'll be free to walk out of this office if she doesn't care for my offer."

Douglas didn't know quite what to say. "As you suggest, I'll need time to think."

The Deputy Commissioner's shrug indicated indifference.

But Douglas was not fooled. "You'll want her as a witness to hang MacLeod."

"Her testimony would be helpful."

"As MacLeod and his people well know. Now I understand why that car tried to run us down in the parking lot two nights ago. The syndicate thinks I'm mixed up in this thing with Eleanor."

"I believe the notion may have occurred to them."

"Maybe Eleanor has the best idea, wanting me to get her to hell out of Hong Kong and up to Tokyo."

Sir Frederick shook his head. "A panic reaction. The syndicate is large, well organized and heavily financed. Their hired killers would find Mrs. Gordon. And you."

"How can I help her? And myself?"

"The Protective Service," Sir Frederick said, "has its own methods of protecting valuable witnesses."

The deal was plain. If Eleanor agreed to work with the Crown and help convict MacLeod, she and Douglas would be provided with bodyguards. Never had the American felt so remote from his New York practice.

"Before I make any decision, Sir Frederick," he said, "I want some legal advice. About smuggling. Domestic relations. Eleanor's position. American immigration laws. And while I'm at it I want the low-down on you and the Protective Service. I'm an alien here, I'm pretty far from home and I'm out of my depth."

The Deputy Commissioner was not offended. "Good advice is always helpful. You'll find a number of first-rate solicitors here. I can recommend several, or, if you prefer, your colleagues at our major hospitals could send you to their attorneys."

"Thanks all the same," Douglas said. "But you're putting pressure on Eleanor and me, some gold-syndicate thugs tried to kill us and the only place I'll get what I need is the U. S. Consulate General."

X

Few American embassies were as large or employed as diversified a staff as the nation's Consulate General, a huge concrete and steel structure located in Hong Kong's Central District. Among them were economists and Chinese scholars, political scientists, sociologists and people who spent their professional lives listening on high-powered radio receiving sets to provincial broadcasts from every part of mainland China. It was rumored, too, but had never been officially confirmed, that the various American intelligence-gathering agencies were well represented. Certainly it was no secret that the establishment was a China-watching station without equal, and not even the presence of the small American mission in Peking diminished its usefulness and importance.

The problems created by bureaucratic red tape that permeated the government were evident in some departments, and Douglas Gordon was shunted from one section to another, telling his story to polite officials who were mildly sympathetic but expressed an inability to advise him. He persisted, however, and finally found the man he was seeking.

The name plate on his desk identified him as L. F. Martin, an assistant commercial attaché, but an Interpol directory and a Hong Kong Preventive Service chain-of-command chart taped to a wall indicated that his actual role might be other than it seemed. A gray-haired man in a rumpled seersucker suit who chain-smoked and frequently polished his horn-rimmed glasses as he listened to his visitor's narrative, he neither interrupted nor asked questions.

"That," Douglas concluded, "is where I stand, Mr. Martin. According to Sir Frederick Simpson my wife is a crook, but he made it plain she won't be prosecuted if she'll act as a Crown witness when her former confederates are rounded up. The picture is ugly, and I want some advice. For me. And for Eleanor."

Martin lighted a cigarette. "I've already checked you out, Dr. Gordon, and what you've told me about yourself tallies with the file that Washington put together in a hurry when I requested information on you. So I know you're giving me a straight account, and that helps."

"Hold on a minute," Douglas said. "May I ask why you wanted a background report on me?"

The older man shrugged. "Oh, we hear things, so we like to be prepared. We don't look or act like Boy Scouts, but old Dan Beard's motto is in our blood."

"Obviously," Douglas said, "Sir Frederick got in touch with you after my first meeting with him."

"Don't take offense, Doctor. This department has a job to do."

"Just what is the department?"

The official did not reply, and shifted ground. "Not many surgeons your age have built up a reputation as good as yours, and you have a first-class military record, too. So you're too distinguished a guy to be getting mixed up in some seamy business. If you've come to me for advice I can give it to you in three simple words. Go home. Now."

"Maybe I will, once I have a better understanding of the stakes. Sir Frederick has an ax to grind, but presumably you don't, and that's why I've come to you. I'd like a clarification of my wife's position."

"That brings up a point that you may think is none of my business, but it is. You and Mrs. Gordon lived apart for six years, but you suddenly show up here brandishing a sword and shield as her protector. Are you?"

Douglas knew what he was asking, and saw no reason to mince words. "We've resumed marital relations, if that's what you want to know, Mr. Martin."

The official removed his glasses, held them to the light and removed an invisible smudge. "That makes a difference in your legal as well as your personal situation."

"Eleanor is my wife in fact as well as name. Is that what you're saying?"

"Precisely, Doctor."

"Okay, suppose I can persuade her to come to New York with me. It's the only sensible thing for her to do when a gang of gold smugglers is after her and the Preventive Service is breathing down her neck. I'd like answers to two hypothetical questions. Am I right in assuming that, as the wife of an American citizen, she'd be granted a visitor's visa—at the very least? And is there anything Sir Frederick could or would do to block her departure from Hong Kong once he learned she was washing her hands of the mess here?"

"The visa division," Martin said, "gives sympathetic priority to the husbands or wives of citizens. The usual procedure is for the spouse to enter the United States on a visitor's visa, which can be extended from time to time. They initiate their applications for citizenship, and are then required—under the law—to leave and reenter the country in order to qualify for permanent residence. Ordinarily this means a quick trip to Canada or Mexico."

"Sounds simple."

"It is, Doctor. As for Sir Frederick, I'm in no position to know his mind, and I have no idea how important Mrs. Gordon might be in the case he's building. Speaking purely technically, if he wanted to prevent her from leaving Hong Kong he could get a court order authorizing the Preventive Service to pick up her passport. I can't tell you whether he'd go that far."

"It's a risk we'll have to take. I've got to get Eleanor out of here."

"You appear determined."

"I am, Mr. Martin," Douglas said. "I've just learned of my wife's involvement in a gold-smuggling ring, but I'm damned if I'm going to see her whole life ruined because she once acted as a gold courier. She was very young, and she must have been under great pressures—financial, whatever—to accept that kind of work. It's behind her now, and I earn enough to make sure she won't have to work for a living. I'm even intending to persuade her, if I can, to give the Crown Colony government any funds she may have accumulated. That kind of gesture ought to prove her good faith and make it very difficult for the Preventive Service to take away her passport."

"That's a clever idea, Doctor. Congratulations for dreaming up a new twist. I've seen all kinds over the years here."

"You think it might work?"

"You won't want to hear what I think, Dr. Gordon. I'm sorry to tell you this, but I'm convinced nothing will persuade Mrs. Gordon to go to the United States with you."

Douglas stared at him. "What do you know that I don't, Mr. Martin?"

Again the official polished his glasses. "You may or may not realize that very little gold has been smuggled in or out of the United States for more than a generation. It's one of the few major crimes we've been spared. For one thing, our own production of raw gold, even in Alaska, has been reduced to an insignificant trickle. Even more important has been the law prohibiting private citizens from owning gold bullion. It hasn't been profitable for the syndicates to offer gold for sale on the black market. Even now that the law has been repealed."

Douglas felt a surge of impatience. "Get to the point, please."

"Believe me, I am. About ten years ago one of the syndicates proved to be sharper than the others, and realized there was an untapped market in Central America. There are very few direct flights to those countries from overseas, and the easiest way to reach them was to fly to the U.S. and change planes. So that's the system they worked out—and utilized successfully."

"What are you trying to tell me?"

"Eleanor Chang—more recently known as Eleanor Chang Gordon—was employed by the syndicate as a courier on that route, and made a number of such trips, traveling in transit through the United States. So she's wanted for questioning by the customs and several other federal agencies. She wasn't a big enough fish for us to ask for her extradition, but I guarantee you she'll be nabbed the day she sets foot on American soil. *What's more, she knows it.* She was a professional for a long time, and she realizes that couriers get ten-year sentences in federal penitentiaries when they're caught."

Douglas felt as though he had been kicked in the stomach.

"I'm sorry to do this to you, Doctor, but I figured you'd blunder into even worse trouble than you're in if you didn't know the score. I'd show you the lady's dossier if I could. I had Washington send it along to me, too, but it carries a restricted label, so I can just pass along the essence."

"I don't need to see it, thanks." Douglas spoke quietly, trying to sort out his feelings, but suddenly they overwhelmed him, and to his own surprise, he lost his temper. "I've had it!" he shouted, pounding the desk. "A gang of crooks, headed by my wife, have made a damn idiot out of me. They've taken advantage of my instincts, my sentiment for the past, even my profession. I'm finished!"

The official tried to interrupt, but could not halt the torrent.

"I've never struck a woman in my life, but I'd like to beat the hell out of Eleanor! And everybody connected with her! Including the double-talking Hong Kong police! Ah, nuts to it—I'm taking your advice, and I'm going home. I'm getting back to New York on the first airplane!"

"Don't," Martin said.

Douglas was so astonished he could only stare at the man.

"I asked you, officially, to get back to the States. Now, strictly off the record, I'm urging you to stay on in Hong Kong and see this business through to the end."

"Which of us has gone crazy?" Douglas demanded.

"Neither," Martin said. "I shouldn't be telling you this, and I'll deny it if you ever quote me, but you're a dead man if you go back to New York now."

"I'm sick of this run-around!"

"Sure you are," Martin said. "But you've been dragged into a very nasty mess. And like it or not, you're in it up to your neck. You know just enough to be dangerous to some unscrupulous, powerful people. They won't become involved directly, but they'll get rid of you on a contract job. Cash on the line to professional killers, and that's the end of a prominent surgeon."

Douglas saw he was serious, and made an effort to think clearly. "I know nothing about these things, but it seems to me they could shoot me down anywhere."

"True enough. But you're safer in Hong Kong than you'd be anywhere else, even though the Preventive Service and the police would like to wash their hands of you. As long as you stay on here, while they're making a concerted effort to break a case wide open, they're obliged to protect you. They *must*. I won't say you're really safe in Hong Kong, Doctor, but you're better off here than you'd be in New York. The local authorities would have my head on a platter if they knew I was telling you this, and my own bosses wouldn't be any too happy. But I don't want the murder of a nice guy on my conscience."

"But I'm so disgusted with—"

"Wouldn't you rather be disgusted than dead?" Martin asked, and escorted him to the door.

A few moments later Douglas reached the street, but was unaware of the stifling heat and the glare of the sun. At last he understood why Eleanor had refused from the outset to go with him to the United States, and he was badly shaken. He wanted to tell her he knew her whole story, and he felt an overpowering desire to get out of Hong Kong. Martin had been in earnest, however, and his advice was worth pondering. The preservation of his life was even more important than the recovery of his self-esteem.

Douglas crossed the square in front of the Consulate General and started off toward his hotel, a few blocks away. The crowds were appreciably thinner, and he realized it was noon, the one time of day when Hong Kong's millions had the good sense not to expose themselves to the sun. The city had become a modern metropolis in the years since World War II, but in this one respect it clung to its nineteenth-century habits, when only polo players, golf enthusiasts and other sports-loving Anglo-Saxons had ventured out of doors during the most uncomfortable period of the day.

An automobile pulled to a halt at the curb only a few feet from Douglas, but he paid no attention to it until he heard someone call, "Dr. Gordon!"

The speaker was a blond, well-tailored young man who sat in the back seat of a limousine driven by a uniformed Chinese.

Reacting automatically, Douglas moved toward the open window.

"I hate to impose on your good nature or your time, Dr. Gordon," the young man said in a cultured English accent, "but my employer is eager to meet you. I wonder if I might take you to him. He asked me to assure you he'll be grateful for a brief chat."

The driver left his post at the wheel, walked around the car and unobtrusively opened the rear door.

"Who is your employer?"

"Mr. Ian MacLeod."

Douglas felt a stab of fear, and hesitated. It would be wise if he told the manager of his hotel where he was going and then let this overly amiable young man know what he had done. The precaution might discourage any tendency on the part of syndicate members to resort to violence. "I'll be delighted to meet Mr. MacLeod," he said, "but I want to stop off first at my hotel for telephone messages."

"That won't be necessary," the young man said. "We'll soon have you back at the hotel. Meantime you can always call them from Mr. MacLeod's house."

The driver was standing only a pace from Douglas, who saw he had a hand in a pocket of his uniform jacket that bulged. Although it was unlikely that he would use firearms, even assuming he was actually carrying a gun, it was best to take no chances. Douglas stepped into the car.

The young man offered him an English cigarette from a gold case. "Mr. MacLeod is sensitive to favors," he said, still bland. "He'll be most appreciative."

The car moved away from the curb, its engine silent, and Douglas realized he could disappear without a trace. "I'm glad," he said, his smile wry, "that I can oblige him with so little effort."

The young man settled back against the leather upholstery. "I don't suppose you'd know that skyscraper under construction over there is going to be the new MacLeod Building."

"Very impressive."

"We think of it as a convenience. Our offices are scattered all over the Island and Kowloon, and we'll be able to function far more efficiently when we've consolidated all of our departments under one roof."

Douglas made the effort to keep up his end of the conversation. "How soon will you move in?"

"We're scheduled to occupy it in three months, but we'll be lucky if it's finished in six. These bloody colonials bear down only when they're working for themselves, and then they labor like their coolie ancestors. We've been here for over one hundred and fifty years, mind you, but they still think of the English as foreigners who deserve to be cheated."

The hatred that crept into his voice when he spoke of Hong Kong's natives was so intense that Douglas was surprised. His air of imperturbability was only a thin veneer, it seemed. "You prefer doing business in London, then." It did no harm to probe.

"Vastly. But when Mr. MacLeod travels, I travel, so here I am. I'm looking forward to a holiday of salmon fishing in Scotland, so I'm hoping he'll clean up some odds and ends here without too many delays."

They were following the waterfront road, one of the city's principal thoroughfares, and after leaving the Central District and Wanchai behind, the limousine picked up speed.

The young man, who apparently missed nothing, saw Douglas taking note of their surroundings. "We'll be there shortly," he said. "Mr. MacLeod hates to waste time, and refuses to live more than twenty minutes' drive from his office."

The limousine turned inland just before reaching a small bathing beach, and after passing several expensive high-rise apartment buildings turned onto a dirt road. Bamboo thickets and other tropical foliage grew tall, making it impossible to see the private homes that stood on large sites, and the abrupt change from the crowded highway was startling. In seconds the car had moved into another world.

The driver slowed to a crawl, and in a few minutes came to a halt before an open-work grille set in a towering mass of bamboo. A slender Cantonese gateman saluted, then opened the grille, and the limousine moved up a long, winding driveway of gravel. There were flower beds lining it on both sides, and the immaculately tended lawn reminded Douglas of a putting green.

Ahead stood a sprawling three-story building of gray fieldstone that resembled an English manor house, and beyond it the American caught a glimpse of a swimming pool and two tennis courts. Even by the standards of Hong Kong's upper crust the place was impressive.

They stopped at the massive front door, but the young man led Douglas down a gravel path to a screened porch that looked out on the swimming pool. The room was enormous, and potted plants and flowers were everywhere, giving it the appearance of a greenhouse.

"I'll tell Mr. MacLeod you're here," the young man said, and vanished.

Rather than sit on one of the cushioned wrought-iron chairs Douglas wandered through the miniature jungle. He saw orchids of several varieties, pink and white camellias and two huge gardenia bushes that should have been planted outdoors. There were other blooming flowers, too, that he failed to recognize, and unexpectedly he came upon a large tank stocked with colorful striped fish.

"I think tiger fish are such fun, don't you?" a woman asked in a pronounced English accent.

Douglas turned and saw an exceptionally tall redhead with a fair complexion and expertly done makeup that emphasized her green eyes. She was wearing an open sleeveless terrycloth robe over a bikini that did justice to her figure, and on the hand she held out to the American was a single piece of jewelry, a very large emerald and diamond ring. In spite of her beach attire her skin was pale, indicating that she avoided the sun. He guessed she was in her early thirties.

"You must be Dr. Gordon," she said. "I'm Daphne MacLeod." She studied him, her eyes guarded in spite of her smile of welcome.

Her hand was cool, he noted, her grip firm and rather masculine.

"Ian had to take an overseas telephone call, but he won't be long. Would you like a pink gin while we're waiting?" She moved to a bar half concealed by a five-foot-high miniature banana palm.

Douglas found it almost possible to forget that he was here only because the chauffeur had threatened him with a hidden pistol. "I'm afraid I've never developed a taste for pink gin, thank you."

She prepared herself a drink, and her laugh was apologetic. "Then fix yourself anything that strikes your fancy. I'd do it for you, but I'm not much of a bartender, and I always get the proportions wrong."

She had such an air of authority that he refused to believe she was inefficient in anything she did. On the verge of refusing the offer, he saw no reason to deny himself, and joined her at the bar.

Daphne made no move out of his way, and her arm touched his.

He was surprised to see two bottles of Bourbon, a whiskey consumed almost exclusively by Americans, and poured himself a mild drink, filling his glass with ice and water. He didn't know what lay ahead, and wanted his mind clear.

She drifted to the far side of the porch, lowered herself into a wrought-iron chair and waved him into another opposite her.

Her robe was completely open now, inviting him to admire her figure, and he did. She was about five or six years older than Eleanor, he estimated, and although no man was entirely predictable, he was inclined to believe Sir Frederick had been right when he'd said that MacLeod was faithful to her. She was the sort of woman who would occupy the full attention and energies of any man.

"You've been seeing the sights, I suppose," she said.

"Not on this trip. I've only been here a short time, and I've been rather busy."

"I didn't realize you knew Hong Kong. When were you last here?"

Douglas had no idea whether she was making small talk to keep him occupied, but he saw no harm in playing the game. "About six years ago."

"There are so many new buildings constantly under construction that I sometimes wonder if I'm in New York or Houston."

It was apparent, he thought, that she had traveled in the United States.

"I spend several months out here every spring and summer," she said, "and the transformation of the skyline has been astonishing in the nineteen years Ian and I have been married."

"Nineteen years? You must have been a child bride."

"I was rather young." A dimple appeared in her left cheek when she smiled. "And you're gallant to say so, Doctor."

She was flirting with him, he knew, but couldn't imagine her motive, even while feeling certain that every change of expression, every gesture, was deliberate.

"You must come round again for a few sets of tennis," she said. "I always play in the late afternoon, when the sun is less intense. We'll make a definite date before you leave."

Douglas hadn't played in years, but kept that information to himself. Tennis was her excuse, not her reason, yet he doubted that she was rash enough to be inviting a total stranger to an intimate rendezvous. He replied vaguely, uncertain of her involvement in whatever plots the gold-smuggling syndicate might be hatching.

A door opened, and Ian MacLeod, crisp in white trousers, shoes and sports shirt, crossed the porch in a few strides. He was a bearded, barrel-chested giant who crushed the visitor's hand in a powerful grip, and his booming voice filled the room. "My London office infuriates me," he said, a hint of a Scottish burr in his accent. "The bloody fools won't wipe their noses without permission. Forgive me for keeping you waiting, Dr. Gordon."

"I was charming him," Daphne said, "and he didn't miss you, darling."

Her husband dismissed her with a gesture. "I'm here now."

She pouted, but rose to her feet without delay, and before departing handed him a pink gin. "I fixed this for you as a reward for your patience with London on the telephone," she said. "Don't let Dr. Gorden leave without setting a tennis date with me." She smiled at Gordon, then drifted away.

"Don't change just yet, Daph," her husband called after her. "We'll have a quick swim before lunch."

Their relationship, Douglas told himself, was complicated.

MacLeod dropped onto a cushioned sofa. "Very good of you to come, Dr. Gordon."

Douglas dropped all pretense of civility. "I'm here because I was given no choice."

The Scotsman looked shocked. "Oh, dear. I hope Dennis and the chauffeur weren't rude."

"They were painfully polite—after making it clear that the driver was prepared to use a gun he was carrying."

"One's employees so often fail to show finesse," MacLeod murmured. "I've discovered it takes years to train them properly." He studied the American as he sipped his drink. "I've been hearing a great deal about you in recent days, Dr. Gordon."

"The same to you," Douglas said, "although I'd never heard of you until I got here."

"I share your annoyance over the trick Eleanor used to bring you here. That sort of shabbiness is beneath her."

Douglas decided to take the offensive in the hope of catching the man off balance. "Oh, that was mild compared to the story she told me when I saw her. She said she's been your mistress for years, and she was afraid you'd kill her in a fit of jealousy."

The heavy-set man's roar of laughter made some delicate ferns tremble. "Her father and brother were incorrigible, too. The curse of the Changs has always been an overly active imagination. I hope you know better, Doctor."

"I do. Now."

"Daphne would put a knife in me if I looked at another woman, as much as she enjoys her own harmless romps. What's the latest product of Eleanor's imagination, may I ask?"

"I imagine she's run out of stories. Because I've pieced together the truth."

MacLeod tugged at his beard, his eyes narrowing.

"My own imagination is limited," Douglas said, "so I know an incident that took place the other night was real. A car tried to run me down in a parking lot, and unless I'm very much mistaken the driver works for you, Mr. MacLeod."

The Scotsman sighed. "Some members of my staff are inclined to be crude, particularly when they act on their own initiative in the hope of winning my approval. I'm relieved you weren't hurt, Dr. Gordon, and I can assure you, now that I'm in Hong Kong, there will be no repetition of such tactics."

"I've been learning a new kind of wariness these past few days," Douglas said.

"I gather you've been learning many things on visits to Sir Frederick Simpson and Larry Martin at the American Consulate."

"You keep well informed." In spite of his calm front Douglas grew taut. The man was keeping tabs on him and knew too damn much.

"My business is like any other, and I have no magic success formula," MacLeod said. "I achieve my ends by avoiding surprises, which means I employ people who keep me fully informed. That brings us to the present. I can imagine what you've gleaned about me, Dr. Gordon, which doesn't worry me. Many people here, in London and elsewhere have heard similar rumors—which can't be proved. What interests me is your intentions."

"I hope," Douglas said, "to resume the practice of surgery in New York. In the immediate future."

"Splendid, but I was referring to your intentions regarding me, Doctor."

"I have none."

"Really?"

"See here, Mr. MacLeod. I'm not a policeman. I'm not a detective. I'm not an undercover agent for the Hong Kong Preventive

Service, the U. S. Treasury Department or any other bureau of any government. If you're mixed up in a gold-smuggling syndicate, that's your business. And the business of the law enforcement people. It has nothing to do with me. I wouldn't raise a hand either to help you or hurt you, and I don't give a hang whether they catch you or you escape. So call off your troops, and keep them called off. All I want is to be left alone."

"A concise statement of your position, Dr. Gordon, and I admire the clarity of your presentation." MacLeod's broad smile indicated approval.

Douglas didn't care what he thought or felt. "Just so we understand each other."

"Indeed we do, so far. Would you care for another drink?"

"No, thanks. I'd like to use your telephone and call for a taxi. I want to attend to some personal matters before I leave Hong Kong."

"I can't allow you to think me inhospitable, so I insist you allow me to put my car and chauffeur at your disposal."

"Just as easy as having me followed, I suppose."

MacLeod ignored the jab. "This gives us an additional moment or two, and your personal affairs happen to be very much on my mind. You're Eleanor's husband, and you spent last night at her flat, so you're very much involved in her future, and that's what interests me. I'll appreciate hearing your plans for her."

"Even if they were decided," Douglas said, his voice rising, "I'm damned if I tell them to you or anyone else. My first order of business is to have a talk with Eleanor. And any conclusions we reach will be strictly private."

MacLeod spread his oversized hands in a gesture of defeat. "I can't blame you for putting me in my place, Dr. Gordon. But there are hidden dangers you know nothing about. Neither does Eleanor. I believe I can do a great deal to explain your joint situation so you'll be able to reach your decisions more easily. So I suggest both of you meet me for cocktails this evening. On board my boat. Eleanor will know how to get there."

"What would prevent you from throwing us overboard?"

MacLeod was amused. "I have an aversion to violence that even the authorities know and appreciate, Doctor. What's more, you have capable protectors. A Preventive Service plainclothesman is tailing you, and so is a security agent from the American Consulate General."

XI

Ian MacLeod's chauffeur knew the address of Eleanor's apartment building without being told, and Douglas realized his wife's situation was even more critical than he had known. If she still thought she could leave Hong Kong unscathed merely by joining him on a flight to Tokyo he would have to disabuse her of the idea. But he could make no decisions for her; she alone would determine her future.

His own agitation was so great that he did not announce himself when he reached the building. Instead he went straight to the flat, the staff members in the lobby greeting him as though he were a permanent resident.

Eleanor, fully made up but clad only in a housecoat and mules, was so relieved to see him that she had to blink away tears. "I've been calling your hotel for hours. I couldn't imagine what happened to you, and I've been afraid for you."

"I've had a busy morning—on your behalf," he said. "I've seen Sir Frederick Simpson, I had a meeting with an official at the U. S. Consulate General who seems to be an expert on gold syndicates and I've just now come from a session with Ian MacLeod, who requested an interview with me at gunpoint."

Eleanor collapsed into a chair.

"I believe I know the whole story," Douglas told her, "including the reason you've always refused to go to America."

She averted her gaze while she composed herself, then looked straight at him. "You have no cause to believe me, Doug, but you'll never know how sorry I am. I wanted you to know everything, but I didn't have the courage to tell you. And you can't imagine how frustrating it is to keep paying for mistakes I made when I was young."

"I'm not sure I follow you."

"You weren't told my background?"

He shook his head.

"You've learned all the rest, so there's no reason to hide it. My father worked in a government bureau in Peking, and when the Reds came to power in Forty-nine we left before he could be arrested. I was very little then, but I remember every detail of our flight. He could have gone to Taiwan with the Nationalists, but he'd become disillusioned with Chiang Kai-shek and preferred exile in Hong Kong. My mother died soon after we arrived here."

She spoke in a monotone, not seeking sympathy, but Douglas couldn't help feeling sorry for her.

"My father and my brother—who is twelve years older than I—faced the problem of earning a living. I don't know how they were recruited by the syndicate, but my father became a local contact man and my brother went to work as a courier. I was still in school when my father died, and as soon as I was old enough I was taken into the organization and trained as a courier, too. It seemed natural, and the thought of doing anything else never occurred to me."

She had been doomed since childhood, Douglas thought, and his heart went out to her.

"I earned a good living, much more than I could have made in any legitimate enterprise. But I became frightened and dissatisfied when my brother was taken by the police in Manila and sent to prison. They're very strict, and he's still there. That was a little more than eight years ago, and I was looking for some way out, some way to change my whole pattern, when you came into my life."

She was making no excuses, he realized, and was telling her tale without embellishment.

"At first I saw you as a means of escape, and then I fell in love with you," Eleanor said. "Not until months after we were married did I discover it wouldn't be safe for me to go to the United States. So I solved none of my problems by marrying you. All I succeeded in doing was to become emotionally involved with you and make an even worse mess of my life."

Acting on sudden impulse, Douglas went to her and put a hand on her shoulder.

A moment later she was in his arms, clinging to him.

He felt her tremble, and knew he could not abandon her. It was impossible for him to return to New York, walking out of her life when she so desperately needed him.

"Tell me what to do," she said.

He lowered her to the divan, then sat opposite her so her proximity wouldn't interfere with his ability to think clearly. "You're in a bad spot because you're caught between opposing forces, both of them tough. MacLeod wants to make certain you'll keep your mouth shut about him and the people who work for him. Sir Frederick wants you to become a Crown witness because he appears to believe your testimony will send MacLeod to prison and badly cripple the syndicate."

"It serves me right for writing the letter," Eleanor said.

"What letter?"

"Sir Frederick didn't tell you about it? I tried to quit the syndicate, but Ian wouldn't hear of it. I begged and I threatened, but he wouldn't listen. I was the best courier they had, and they wouldn't let me retire. I became so angry and upset that I sent an anonymous letter to the Preventive Service, naming Ian and everyone else in the organization I knew. That's when I suddenly found myself in the middle of a tug of war."

"I see."

"I'm sure Sir Frederick knows I wrote that letter, and so does Ian. They're like two English bulldogs. They've sunk their teeth into me, and neither of them will let me go."

"MacLeod has shown you his intentions by trying to have you killed in the parking lot. He tried to convince me his people were acting without orders, but I don't believe him."

"Neither do I," Eleanor said, and shuddered.

Douglas reached out to stroke her hand. "Sir Frederick made it plain to me that he'll assign you bodyguards if you'll tell your story in court."

"What good would that do me?" she demanded. "Suppose they were able to protect me, which is a flimsy supposition because Ian is far more clever than all the Preventive Service top brass. I'd still be sent to prison myself for having been a courier."

"Not necessarily," he said. "Sir Frederick hinted he'd ask the court to deal leniently with you."

"Crown justices are less inclined to make deals than your American courts."

"Perhaps, but I may have found a way to soften the bench still more. If you were to make restitution—out of the large sums you've made as a courier—I find it difficult to believe that any judge would send you to prison."

Eleanor stared at him for a moment, then laughed without humor. "You're hopelessly naïve, Doug. Do you really believe I've put away a fortune?"

"Well, Sir Frederick gave me an idea of what you've made, and ten percent of every smuggling operation adds up to an appreciable sum."

She laughed again. "Of course it does. I've been paid handsomely, but I've lived according to my means. Perhaps you haven't heard that rents are higher in Hong Kong than in any other city on earth. And payoffs to the police and minor Preventive Service people have kept me out of trouble, but they've been enormously expensive. I did my last job as a courier two years ago, and my assets have been dwindling. In another year and a half they'll be gone. So I couldn't offer enough in restitution to interest even a traffic court judge."

"So much for that idea, but I still think you have no real alternative. Neither the syndicate nor the Preventive Service would stand aside while you flew off to Tokyo or Taipei with me."

"You're wrong," Eleanor said. "Now that you've become involved and Ian knows you've been in touch with the Preventive Service, he won't want anything unpleasant to happen to either of us. He'll be afraid the violence will be traced back to him, and he won't place himself in that kind of jeopardy. He's spent his whole career keeping his hands clean."

"But Sir Frederick won't let you leave."

"He will, Doug. He has no choice. If he has me arrested I'll refuse to testify on the grounds that I might incriminate myself, and he knows it. Rather than give up his case against Ian, his real target, he'll have his undercover people keep me under surveillance. I'm positive no one will try to stop us when we go on board that airplane!"

He shook his head. "Your idea is self-defeating in the long run. The syndicate will keep you under observation wherever you go, and so will the law."

"No," she said, and her voice hardened. "What you fail to realize is that Hong Kong is a tiny place. It isn't easy to hide in an area of less than four hundred square miles. In Japan, I can shake off a whole crowd that may be trailing me, I don't care how many of them there might be."

"But you can't stay in hiding forever," Douglas said.

"I don't intend to. You haven't heard the rest of my plan. I have friends—people who owe me favors—in several of the Central American republics. I can go there, probably by way of Rio de Janeiro, and they'll give me a safe place of refuge for as long as I want it. You can visit me there whenever you please, whenever you can take time from your practice. And in a year and a half, at just about the time my money gives out, the U.S. statute of limitations against me will expire. The Americans won't be able to press charges against me, and I'll finally be able to join you in New York and live as your wife!"

Her ingenuity, he thought, was boundless. "Clever."

"I've had a long time to work out a foolproof scheme, Doug. I don't intend to be trapped. Not by Sir Frederick, not by Ian."

"You'll have your chance to prove it. Sooner than you think. MacLeod has invited us to have cocktails with him today, on his boat."

"A command performance. How lovely!" Eleanor sat erect, eager to meet the challenge. "I've been waiting a long time to face him as an equal. I won't be going as Eleanor Chang, courier, but as Mrs. Douglas Gordon, and that makes all the difference in the world."

They parked Eleanor's convertible near a small inlet that faced the outer islands, and at first glance the area seemed almost deserted. Smoke was rising from the chimney of a small house on the inner side of the shore road, and a junk anchored a half mile from shore tugged at its line in the early-evening tide. The place was so isolated it appeared to be miles instead of mere yards from civilization, and Douglas felt a stab of apprehension.

"We should have told the police or the Preventive Service where we were going," he said.

Eleanor relaxed behind the wheel and lighted one of her slender cigarettes. "Ian wouldn't appreciate that."

"We're perfect ambush targets, which I wouldn't appreciate."

She dismissed his fears with a nonchalant wave. "Ian doesn't operate that way, as you'll see. He wants to meet us so he can make us an offer of some sort, and he won't take any action—subtle action, at that—until he learns our reaction. Besides, he must know we're being trailed by the Preventive Service and your friends from the American Consulate. Two cars that were behind us on the road are parked just beyond those bushes."

"I wasn't even aware of them."

"You haven't spent the better part of your life working outside the law."

Before Douglas could reply they heard the sound of an outboard motor, and a sampan cut into the cove at an angle. It was manned by two brawny Chinese, and when it came closer Douglas saw that both carried pistols in shoulder holsters.

Eleanor threw away her cigarette and left the car. "They're here," she said. "Let's go."

Douglas followed her to a small wharf that jutted into the placid water, and when the sampan moved alongside they jumped onto the deck. The outboard motor roared, and the nose of the little craft rose as she headed toward the junk.

Again the American felt a twinge of uneasiness, but a glance at Eleanor reassured him. She stood amidships, balancing without strain, and her face reflected the calm of a young woman enjoying an ordinary outing with her husband. She exchanged no words with the two Chinese, and seemingly was unaware of their existence; they, in return, paid no attention to their passengers.

Even at a distance of only a few yards the junk resembled scores of others, and Douglas wondered why Ian MacLeod would use such a shabby fishing vessel as headquarters of some sort. A seaman in a nondescript shirt and trousers lowered a rope ladder, one of the men in the sampan stretched it taut and Eleanor began to climb to the deck above, her progress in no way impeded by her high heels.

Douglas followed close behind her, and a glimpse of the deck told him this was no ordinary junk. An intricate radar antenna was camouflaged by clothes ostensibly left out to dry, and a long instrument panel was visible inside the glass-enclosed wheelhouse. Douglas suspected the ship was diesel-powered, and that it was equipped with a two-way radio.

Eleanor displayed her familiarity with the junk by going directly to a hatch, and Douglas remained only a pace from her. They descended a short flight of wooden stairs and suddenly were transported into the modern world. The cabin was large, with books lining the bulkheads, and the overstuffed leather furniture was reminiscent of a manor house library.

Daphne MacLeod, dazzling in a short sequin-laden dress, came forward to greet the guests, but barely wasted a nod on Eleanor. "We meet again," she said to Douglas, and took his hand in both of hers.

Her husband, now wearing yachting attire, came in from an adjoining cabin and made it his business to shake hands with both of the newcomers.

A white-coated servant appeared with a tray of hot canapés, another brought drinks, and Douglas noted that he was served a Bourbon and water without having asked for it. MacLeod did not exaggerate when he boasted that no detail was beneath his attention.

"This is an unusual junk," Douglas said.

His host was pleased. "Rather. We use it only for entertaining and short pleasure cruises, much to the chagrin of the Preventive Service. They've boarded us hundreds of times, but they've yet to find an ounce of contraband gold."

One of the lures of his smuggling operations, Douglas realized, was the challenge of outwitting the authorities, of being a long step ahead of everyone else. Eleanor seemed to react in the same way, so perhaps the trait was common to syndicate members.

Daphne continued to flirt with Douglas. "You never told me you had such an attractive husband, Eleanor."

"You never asked."

Both women were bristling, and it was evident to Douglas that there was no love lost between them.

But Ian MacLeod was in no mood for a feminine sparring match. "By now," he said, "I'm sure you've had time to discuss your joint situation and the options open to you."

Douglas hoped his shrug was noncommittal.

But Eleanor was ready for combat. "I don't work for you any longer, Ian, as you well know, and my husband has always been independent. So what we do is strictly our own concern."

MacLeod stroked his beard. "To be sure, my dear, provided your activities don't involve others. One never knows when you might feel the urge to write another letter."

"I was very annoyed at the time," she said, a hint of the defensive creeping into her voice. "But there was no harm done. The Crown prosecutor couldn't prove I wrote it, and I'm sure I didn't tell Sir Frederick anything he didn't already know."

Douglas came to his wife's rescue. "Eleanor and I are planning on a future together in New York."

"I'm hoping to visit New York soon," Daphne said. "I'll ring you for an examination."

MacLeod ignored the digression. "You're talking rubbish, Doctor, and you know it. Eleanor would be arrested before she could clear your immigration authorities."

"Maybe not, Mr. MacLeod."

Eleanor showed her irritation. "We're minding our own business, Ian, and we expect you to do the same!"

"I deeply regret the unfortunate fact that your business is also mine." The Scotsman sipped his pink gin, a hint of force behind his jovial manner.

"I can understand your worry," Douglas said. "You're afraid Eleanor knows too much about certain elements of your past, and in a sense I can't blame you. I'd be a bit uneasy, too. But we've cleared away our own misunderstandings, and I can imagine no reason why you and she should ever cross paths again."

"Spoken like an honest man who has nothing to hide, Doctor," MacLeod said. "I'm sure you meant every word, as honorable men usually do. But I've yet to meet the man, honorable or otherwise, who can control his wife. I know I can't, and Eleanor is far more independent than Daphne."

The redhead looked as though she had been insulted.

Douglas realized Eleanor's safety and his own depended on his ability to convince this hardheaded man that he had nothing to fear from them. "I neither know nor care whether you're a highly placed member of a gold syndicate. I'm a surgeon who—"

"Your wife," MacLeod interrupted, "knows far too much about me, and she's already demonstrated she isn't reliable."

"I give you my word—"

"Not good enough, Doctor. No insult intended."

A cold anger welled up in Douglas. "I hope you aren't threatening us, MacLeod. Because you've picked the wrong guy."

The Scotsman's booming laugh was meant to dispel any such notion. "I'm not a bloody fool, Doctor. If anything nasty happens to either of you, Sir Frederick Simpson won't rest until he's sent me to Stanley Prison for the rest of my life. If you've ever seen the inside of the place, as I'm sure you haven't, you'd understand my determination never to be sent there. So you're in no danger, either of you. For the present. There will be no new version of the miscalculation in the parking lot the other night."

Douglas weighed his assertion. "Quite comforting, except for one small matter. What do you mean when you say we're safe for the present?"

"Ah, you've come straight to the heart of the problem." MacLeod rubbed his hands together. "You're my kind, Doctor. We'll reach an understanding yet, you'll see."

Douglas saw that Eleanor didn't like the turn the conversation had taken and was frowning.

"Let's assume," MacLeod said, "that you go back to your New York hospitals, as I'm convinced you wish to do. Let's also assume you're able to perform a miracle of sorts, and persuade the U. S. Treasury agents to forget the past so you can take Eleanor with you. She lives comfortably in New York as the wife of a renowned surgeon, and all is well. But one little corner of her mind continues to buzz. There's a chap who is sometimes in Hong Kong, sometimes in London, who knows so much about her past that he's a constant threat to her security. How does she rid herself of that threat? Very simply. By going to your efficient American authorities and telling them everything she knows, even offering them a bargain to insure her own immunity."

"An interesting scenario," Douglas said, "but faulty."

"Interesting but irrelevant, you mean," MacLeod replied. "Because it will never be acted out. You Americans have a saying that the Lord helps those who help themselves. I've dedicated myself to the principles of that motto."

Eleanor knew he was amusing himself at their expense, and lost her patience. "Come to the point, Ian!"

"Gladly. Doctor, don't fly back to the States via Tokyo. Go by way of Manila, and I'll provide first-class transportation for both of you. Because, as a farewell gesture, I'm asking Eleanor to perform one last service for me. My dear, I want you to act as a courier and carry a final cargo to our friends in Manila."

"You must be mad," Eleanor said. "Not only are the Filipinos very rough, but you may give me away to them in order to end your danger."

"Not at all." MacLeod sounded lofty. "If you were apprehended you'd have all the more reason to testify against me. No, Eleanor, I intend to place you and your husband in a position that will make it impossible for you to tattle on me without hurting yourselves. You'll be a courier, he'll be an accessory, and every move you make will be recorded by witnesses, my witnesses. You know what to do on the assignment, and the danger to you will be minimal, no greater than it's been on any of your previous travels. In fact, you'll be paid the usual fee plus a generous bonus, which should convince you I have your interest at heart."

Douglas rose, his fists clenched. "MacLeod, you're a bastard!"

The Scotsman nodded. "So I've been told by a number of people on various occasions."

"Suppose we reject your outrageous proposal?"

"You won't, Doctor. As a man devoted to restoring others to health you'll want to preserve your own and your wife's. You'll both do as you're told or I won't be responsible for the consequences. You'll leave Hong Kong the day after tomorrow, and it will do you no good to rush to Sir Frederick in the meantime. As Eleanor well knows, the operations of our organization don't depend on any one individual. Directives have already been issued up and down the line, and even if I should be taken into custody by the Preventive Service, Eleanor will perform a final duty as a courier and you'll accompany her. Or take the unpleasant consequences all of us want to avoid."

Daphne rose, her faintly regretful air that of a perfect hostess. "I hope you won't think us inhospitable if we don't offer you another drink," she said, "but we have a dinner engagement with some old-fashioned friends who'll make a fuss if we're as much as five minutes late. And I hope you won't have forgotten me when I call you in New York for that appointment, Dr. Gordon."

Douglas and Eleanor exchanged few words on the sampan ride back to shore. He was seething, finding it hard to concentrate, and he saw that she appeared far away. Finally, after they reached the convertible, he exploded.

"MacLeod really is a madman if he expects us to follow his insane orders!"

Eleanor spoke quietly as she turned the ignition key. "As he told us, he meant every word. Quite literally. He always does."

"If he thinks I'm going to allow you to smuggle a consignment of gold into Manila—while I watch—"

"He's given his orders."

"To hell with him. We'll go straight to Sir Frederick Simpson."

"It's too late tonight, Doug."

"First thing tomorrow morning, then."

Eleanor reached the shore road and sighed as she turned toward the Central District. "He'll set up an appointment with a Crown prosecutor, who'll take my sworn statement and ask endless questions. A secretary will transcribe the interview, and we'll be lucky if copies are ready for me to sign by the end of the day. Then Sir Frederick will have to get a court order for Ian's arrest, which he won't be able to do until the next day. By then—if I'm not in prison—we'll either be on our way to Manila or we'll be dead."

"You're mesmerized by MacLeod because you've obeyed him for so long, but I don't suffer that handicap. I refuse to accept this outrageous—"

"Please, darling, listen to me." She removed a hand from the wheel and touched his arm. "I know how Ian functions, and I was expecting something like this. So I have a few tricks of my own still to play. Tonight we'll pretend we have no problems. We'll have a lovely dinner at a romantic restaurant, and then we'll make love for hours and hours. Tomorrow morning you'll go back to your hotel as though everything were normal and I'll attend to a few errands. I don't trust the telephone any more, so when I'm ready I'll send Ho Fang to fetch you and he'll bring you to—a place where I'll be waiting for you. Then we'll give all of them the slip. Ian, Sir Frederick, everyone. Just you wait, Doug, and you'll see. Trust me to know what I'm doing."

XII

Douglas returned to his hotel after spending the night with Eleanor at her flat. In spite of his misgivings he had reluctantly accepted her plan, telling himself he could still veto her suggestions if her detailed scheme proved too outlandish. He realized she had succeeded in embroiling him in her own complicated situation even though he wanted nothing to do with the machinations of a gold-smuggling syndicate. But she was his wife, and by resuming marital relations with her he had obligated himself to help her to the best of his abilities. His only reservation now was that he would call a halt if asked to break any laws, and he knew that, at the worst, he could extricate himself by taking the first flight to New York.

He sent a cable to Eddie Baker, saying he expected to spend the next two or three days in Hong Kong before returning home. Then, with nothing better to occupy him until Eleanor sent Ho Fang to him with a message telling him where they were to meet, he sent for the day's English-language newspapers. If he needed proof that he was in an alien world, far from home, the local press emphasized his isolation. He could find only tidbits of American and world news, and most columns were devoted to stories about Hong Kong business or recent crimes of violence committed in the Crown Colony. Murders and kidnapings, shootings and stabbings were commonplace, and as Douglas glanced through the papers he was reminded that life in the Orient was cheap. Overpopulation and a degree of poverty unknown in the West produced a fatalism that made the poor relatively indifferent to killing.

One short article caught his eye, and he read it with an interest he would not have shown a few days earlier:

> A cargo of illegal gold bullion worth HK $560,000 was seized last night by the Preventive Service when a patrol boat intercepted a junk, en route from Macao, when it entered the Crown Colony's territorial waters. Five members of the crew were arrested, but their names are not being released pending their interrogation.
>
> A local solicitor, H. V. Lee, who claimed to represent the sailors, appeared on their behalf at the Central District headquarters of the Service. But bail was denied by a night magistrate.
>
> The gold, neatly stacked in one-kilo bars, has been impounded. If the usual procedure is followed, it will become the property of the Hong Kong government. No mention of the cargo was made in the manifest of the junk, which was ostensibly carrying rice and vegetables, and no documents were found on board that identified the ship's owners.

Sir Frederick Simpson was not as helpless as he had indicated, Douglas realized. It was unlikely that the smuggled gold had been seized in a hit-or-miss raid, so the authorities had received a tip from an informer. Hence the Preventive Service knew more about the activities of its foes than Sir Frederick was willing to admit.

The article reinforced Douglas' belief that Eleanor would be wise to cooperate with the government. She had operated outside the law for so long that the very idea of working with the authorities was anathema to her, but it was possible, now that he knew her whole story, that he might be able to persuade her to change her attitude. He intended to try, even though he didn't yet dare allow himself to think in terms of establishing a permanent home in New York with her. There were too many problems to be solved first.

A tap sounded at the door, and an elderly Chinese who wore a bulky padded jacket in defiance of the heat stood on the threshold.

"I—Ho Fang," he said.

Douglas admitted him to the room, thinking that the man's eyes were strangely glazed.

Ho Fang collapsed on the floor and fell unconscious.

A hasty examination revealed that he had been stabbed repeatedly. His shirt and padded jacket were blood-soaked, his pulse was feeble and his breathing was shallow.

He was in immediate need of medical assistance, but Douglas lacked the facilities to do more for him than administer an injection of adrenalin. Calling the hotel manager, he explained the situation, and after requesting the dispatch of an ambulance he telephoned the police and told Chief Inspector Li what had happened.

Douglas accompanied the patient to the hospital and went to the operating room as an observer while an emergency team fought for his life. They did everything for him that would have been done in an American hospital, and Douglas admired their techniques as well as their proficiency. But the old man had suffered a severe shock and had lost so much blood that he failed to respond. His vital signs faltered, and a scant thirty minutes after he was admitted to the operating room he was pronounced dead.

Douglas accompanied his colleagues from the chamber and found Chief Inspector Li waiting for him in the corridor. They went together to a nearby office, where Li offered the American a cigarette. "Tell me your connection with this man. Tell me what happened at your hotel. Think carefully, Doctor, and leave out no details."

Douglas explained Ho Fang's relationship with Eleanor, and after telling the police official that Ho Fang presumably had come to him with a message he had been unable to deliver, he described the wounds that had been inflicted on the patient. "Whoever it was attacked him wanted to make certain he wouldn't talk. I've rarely seen a victim who sustained as many wounds, and it seems miraculous, Inspector, that he could get as far as my hotel room before he collapsed. By rights he should have died wherever it was that the attack occurred."

Li asked a number of questions, occasionally jotting a few words in a notebook. "You think the purpose of the assault was to prevent this man from delivering Mrs. Gordon's message to you?"

"It seems logical, doesn't it? I want to call her and tell her what's happened."

"If you don't mind, Doctor," Li said, "I prefer that we go together to Mrs. Gordon's flat."

Douglas stared at him. "Surely you don't think she was responsible for the attack!"

The Chief Inspector shrugged. "I make no premature judgments," he said, and led the way to his waiting limousine.

Both men were silent on the short drive, and Douglas tried in vain to order his thoughts. It was inconceivable that Eleanor had either assaulted the old man herself or had persuaded others to perform the act on her behalf. Ian MacLeod was necessarily responsible, but why he had resorted to such drastic measures was too much for Douglas to grasp.

When they reached the apartment house Inspector Li questioned the doorman and lobby attendant, addressing both in Cantonese, and they conversed so rapidly that Douglas was unable to make out what they were saying. All he knew was that the official grew increasingly grim.

At last they went upstairs in the elevator, accompanied by the agitated lobby attendant, and at Li's suggestion Douglas unlocked the door with his own keys. As they entered the foyer another shock awaited the American: the flat had been stripped of its furniture and was empty.

They moved from room to room, and nowhere in the place was there any sign that it had been occupied in the recent past. Eleanor's clothes and other personal belongings were gone, and even a bar of soap that had rested in a dish at the side of the bathtub had been removed.

"When were you last here, Dr. Gordon?" the Chief Inspector wanted to know.

"I left at eight o'clock this morning, as I'm sure the doorman can tell you. He hailed a taxi for me."

"He's already verified the statement, thanks."

"What's happened here, Inspector?"

Li sighed. "All I can tell you is that Mrs. Gordon ordered her car and left at nine a.m. Thirty minutes later some men arrived in an unmarked van and took everything."

Their footsteps clattered on the hardwood floors as they retraced their path through the flat. "Isn't there some way you can trace the movers, Inspector?"

"The building employees claim they couldn't identify the men. They'll be questioned, but I'm not hopeful. Members of the working class here never know much when there's trouble. They don't want to become involved for fear of losing their jobs."

"Maybe Ho Fang wasn't the only one who was stabbed. I'm afraid for Eleanor."

"I'll put a couple of my best investigators to work at this end, and we'll see what they uncover. This is no simple case, Dr. Gordon. A man has been murdered, and now a young lady has disappeared. There are ramifications that aren't visible on the surface, so I suggest you and I pay a visit to Preventive Service headquarters."

Sir Frederick Simpson listened to Douglas and Chief Inspector Li, then spent a long time cleaning the bowl of his pipe. "I suppose," he said, "you're having Ian MacLeod questioned?"

"Of course, as a routine procedure," Li said. "But I don't expect to learn anything from him. He'll produce his usual watertight alibi, and it will stand up."

Douglas became angry. "I'm sure that MacLeod is behind everything that's happened. Even though his wife and Eleanor were the only witnesses, he admitted to me that his men tried to run us down in the Kowloon parking lot. And he made no secret of being a gold smuggler. What's more, Eleanor was frightened by him. That was the chief reason she made elaborate escape plans."

The two officials exchanged glances, and Sir Frederick cleared his throat.

But it was the Chief Inspector who broke the silence. "If you knew none of the principals in this case, Doctor, you might suspect that Mrs. Gordon either killed Ho Fang or had him killed and then went underground."

"Impossible!" Douglas' temper continued to rise.

"How so?"

"He had worked for her family in Peking, and she was very fond of him. She told me in so many words that he was the only person in Hong Kong she could trust!"

"Precisely," Sir Frederick said. "But how would she have felt if she'd found out he betrayed her trust? I'm not saying he did, mind you, because I know none of the details. But I wonder how she might have reacted if she'd learned that Ho Fang was secretly in the employ of the gold syndicate."

"Forgive me if I sound naïve," Douglas said, "but I've had to be something of a judge of human nature in my profession, and even though I was unfamiliar with some aspects of my wife's background, I'm convinced I understand her personality. And I'm telling you flatly she would have been incapable of plunging a knife into that old man. Not once, much less seven or eight times!"

"You may be right, Doctor," Li said, "but in our work suppositions aren't good enough. I won't be satisfied until Mrs. Gordon convinces me she didn't have a hand in the murder."

"If she's still alive herself. God knows what may be happening to her while we sit here going round and round!"

"We sympathize with you, Doctor," Sir Frederick said, "and you have our assurances, both personal and professional, that we're already doing everything in our power to dig to the bottom of this matter."

"But you've just now heard about it!"

The Deputy Commissioner of the Preventive Service smiled. "Not at all. Inspector Li's assistant telephoned me while you were on your way here, and we've already alerted our undercover network to locate Mrs. Gordon—dead or alive."

"Finding a missing person in a community as crowded as Hong Kong," Li added, "is very difficult. We have many problems when people disappear by accident. If Mrs. Gordon has vanished deliberately it could be some time before she comes to the surface sufficiently for us to locate her."

"It's my own feeling," Sir Frederick said, "that she's neither been killed nor abducted. MacLeod's syndicate has a great many reasons for wanting her out of the way, but they know they'll be first on our list of suspects, so I don't believe they'll do anything violent here in Hong Kong. MacLeod himself told you the parking lot assault was a mistake, and now that he's arrived from London, I can't see his people repeating their error."

"I hope you're right." Douglas was dubious.

"You've indicated to us," Li said, "that Mrs. Gordon was as anxious to run away from us as from the syndicate. We deplore both her reasoning and her motives, but she very well may have succeeded. At least temporarily."

"At our first meeting, Doctor," Sir Frederick said, "I urged you to wash your hands of a complicated and grimy business. I repeat my recommendation. Go home today, now, on the next airplane out of Hong Kong, and put everything that has happened here out of your mind. You've been meddling in something beyond your scope, something you simply can't handle. The time has come for you to protect yourself."

Douglas glared at him. "I'll grant you I was called here under false pretenses, Sir Frederick, but rightly or wrongly I've been reunited with my wife, and I can't abandon her when she may have been kidnaped and killed—and is herself suspected of having committed a murder. I'm more at home in surgery than a shooting gallery, but my conscience won't allow me to leave without doing everything possible to help Eleanor!"

Again the officials exchanged glances, and to Douglas' surprise, both smiled.

"Good!" Chief Inspector Li said.

Sir Frederick nodded. "We've been hoping you'd adopt that attitude, Dr. Gordon. It simplifies our problem. I've advised you to go home, but you've chosen—of your own volition—to stay. You make our task easier."

"In what way?"

"I trust I'm correct in assuming that Mrs. Gordon arranged her own disappearance. Let's further assume she did as she told you she would, and sent Ho Fang to notify you where she wanted you to meet her. That means Ho Fang was killed by the syndicate, because it will be more difficult for them to eliminate her if you act as her escort when she leaves Hong Kong. For that same reason she'll be anxious to have you go with her."

"Consequently," Li said, "we believe she'll make an attempt to get in touch with you when you fail to appear at the rendezvous."

"We have a free press in Hong Kong," Sir Frederick said, "but the Preventive Service has asked the newspapers—informally, to be sure—to play up the murder of Ho Fang. We hope Mrs. Gordon will see the article and will realize you never received her message. That should increase the pressure on her to make direct, personal contact with you."

"If you want me to act as a decoy for you so you can take her into custody, I can't agree," Douglas said. "I believe in obeying the law, but I can't join a conspiracy against my wife."

"We're not asking for your divided loyalty," Sir Frederick said.

"Go back to your hotel and wait there until Mrs. Gordon gets in touch with you. By telephone, by letter, perhaps in person. Meet her as she suggests, and I'm sure you'll make another attempt to persuade her to cooperate with us."

"I will, but the death of Ho Fang is sure to frighten her, and she'll be more determined than ever to handle things in her own way." Douglas couldn't understand what the authorities wanted him to do.

"We'll station two plainclothesmen in the lobby of your hotel around the clock," Li said. "You'll be followed and protected. So will Mrs. Gordon, even though she doesn't know it. The killers of Ho Fang must be even more desperate than they were, and they won't know you're being guarded. So an attempted assault on you and Mrs. Gordon will not only fail but will also give us a legitimate charge to bring against them."

"Mrs. Gordon is just a small cog in the syndicate machinery," Sir Frederick said. "We won't be too badly upset if she slips out of our grasp—provided we can catch MacLeod, as well as anyone else on his level who lands in our net."

"Call it what you will," Douglas said, "you want me to act as a decoy."

"Have it your way," the Deputy Commissioner of the Preventive Service said with a sigh. "But please understand we're not asking you to do anything that will harm Mrs. Gordon or will interfere with her freedom of choice. Once we can bring charges against MacLeod and make them stick, I don't care where she goes or how she gets there."

Douglas felt cornered, but Eleanor's welfare was still his sole concern, and he knew there was little or nothing he could do to help her if he acted alone. "Okay," he said, "I'll play the game according to your rules, but all bets are off if you try to double-cross my wife."

XIII

Douglas went alone to his hotel, and after notifying the switchboard where he could be reached he ate a quick lunch in the coffee shop. Then, after buying the evening newspapers, he strolled through the lobby to the elevator, wondering which of the men of many nationalities were the plainclothes operatives assigned to protect him. He could not identify them, and they did not reveal themselves, so he had to be content. It was enough, he supposed, to know they were on hand.

The newspapers, as Sir Frederick had indicated, featured the murder of Ho Fang in front-page stories. But Douglas was surprised to find there was no mention of the role he himself had played. The articles stated that the old man had collapsed in a hotel on Hong Kong side, leaving readers with the impression that he had fallen unconscious in the lobby. The uninformed had no way of knowing that he had made his way to the room of an American surgeon but had been unable to deliver the message that had cost him his life.

It was difficult for Douglas to concentrate, and neither the newspapers nor a book could hold his attention. He wandered around his room, pausing occasionally to stare out at the traffic in the harbor, and the afternoon dragged. Not until he actually saw Eleanor would he believe she was safe and unharmed, and the hard knot of apprehension that had formed in the pit of his stomach refused to dissolve. It would be the supreme irony if he lost Eleanor for all time just when they seemed to be on the verge of establishing an enduring relationship.

The ringing of the telephone startled him, and a glance at his watch indicated it was 6 P.M.

"This is Daphne MacLeod," the voice of the cultivated English woman told him. "I'm in the lobby, hoping you'll buy me a drink."

"I'll be right down," he said, and informed the operator where he could be reached if any other calls came in.

Daphne was waiting for him near the bank of elevators. "I've been shopping," she said, charm bracelets jangling as she extended a cool hand, "and on sudden impulse I hoped you'd take pity on me."

Douglas made an appropriate reply as he guided her to the cocktail lounge at the far end of the lobby, but he knew she was lying. She had made up her face within the past half hour and was wearing a revealing dress that would have been inappropriate for a hot afternoon of shopping in crowded stores. Her visit was deliberate, and had been planned with care.

The Eurasian hostess led them to a banquette at the far end of the lounge. The table was situated beyond the range of possible eavesdroppers, and Douglas couldn't help wondering if the hostess had been tipped off in advance and paid for her cooperation. He wasn't becoming paranoid, he assured himself; in his present situation anything was possible.

Daphne discussed the weather and some bargains she had supposedly found on her shopping expedition, but her green eyes became solemn after a waiter had taken their order. "I hope," she said, "you've recovered from your dreadful experience of this morning."

Douglas pretended not to know what she meant.

"That poor old man losing consciousness in your room. You must have known at once, far better than a layman would, that he was in a critical condition."

He still tried to look blank.

"Please, my dear," she said, placing her hand on his arm. "There's no need to put on a show for my benefit. I know."

Aware that she hadn't removed her hand, he took the plunge. "I was wondering how you could have found out," he said, "when there wasn't a single word about me in the newspaper accounts."

"Ian wasn't exaggerating when he told you he keeps well informed. It isn't difficult for him to find out anything he wants to know in Hong Kong."

Douglas hoped his smile was appropriately enigmatic.

The waiter arrived with their drinks, and Daphne allowed her hand to drop.

Douglas waited for her to speak.

She raised her glass in a toast, then addressed him in a low tone. "Poor Eleanor," she murmured. "She did the wrong thing by becoming panicky and running away."

His apprehension lessened somewhat. If the redhead was telling the truth, Eleanor hadn't been injured, kidnaped or killed.

"She ought to know after all these years of doing business with Ian that he wouldn't harm her," Daphne said. "He admits he may have been too strident when he ordered her to take a shipment to Manila tomorrow, but Eleanor should realize that's just his manner."

"He sounded pretty convincing to me," Douglas said.

"But you don't know him as well as Eleanor does. He didn't want to upset either of you, and he's willing to reconsider. In fact, he told me he's sure he can work out an arrangement with you that will satisfy everyone."

"With me?"

"You and Eleanor."

"What kind of an arrangement does he have in mind?"

Daphne sipped her drink. "Ian believes money can solve any problem."

"I can't speak for Eleanor."

"But you can pass the word along when you see her, and I'm sure you'll tell her that Ian hopes to hear from her. Before the deadline he set for tomorrow morning. In some ways he's rather particular, and he hates to have anyone ever gain the mistaken impression that he doesn't keep his word." Daphne's smile seemed to belie the threat.

"You're assuming," Douglas said, "that I'm going to see Eleanor in the near future."

"But Ho Fang must have told you—" She broke off. "Or did he? Ian was wondering whether he delivered Eleanor's message before he collapsed."

"I might be in a better position to answer if I knew what makes MacLeod think Ho Fang planned to give me a message from Eleanor."

"Ian doesn't tell me everything," she said with a pout. "You'd be surprised how often he hurts me by being cryptic—as though he didn't trust me."

She was far more clever than he had thought after their previous meetings, and he began to see her value to MacLeod. "I'm an outsider in all this, but I do have ties to Eleanor," he said. "So I'm in a delicate position."

Again she placed her hand on his arm. "May I tell you something? I hope you'll believe me, because I mean it. Don't try to outsmart Ian. If you're planning on meeting Eleanor somewhere, Ian will learn about it. He already knows the Preventive Service has placed you under surveillance, but his people make the government men look like amateurs."

Douglas tried to strike a light note. "With two groups following me around Hong Kong, I ought to be leading quite a parade."

"Ian will be very grateful for your cooperation, as he'll prove. So will I, for my own reasons." Daphne inched closer to him on the banquette, so her thigh touched his.

"What are your reasons?"

"Ian rewards me whenever I bring him information he wants, and I have my eye on a gorgeous ruby dinner ring."

For the first time, Douglas thought, she was probably telling the truth.

"I can do my own proving, far faster than Ian." She faced him, her eyes limpid. "Tell me whatever you know and I'll go up to your room with you right now."

"Won't MacLeod's men, who are hanging out in the lobby, report back to him what you've done?"

Daphne raised a rounded shoulder, then let it fall again in a pretty display of indifference. "As long as I get the information he wants Ian doesn't care what methods I use."

The moral elasticity of the MacLeod marriage spoke for itself, but Douglas wasn't interested in passing judgment on the couple. Daphne could be dangerous, doubly so if he scorned her, so he had to tread carefully. There was nothing to be gained by pretending he and Eleanor had arranged a time and place for a rendezvous, so he decided a show of truth might be effective. "I wouldn't want to take you to bed without keeping a bargain," he said, "and I can't. Ho Fang delivered no message to me."

She arched an eyebrow.

"He was barely able to tell me his name before he lost consciousness. And if MacLeod is as well informed as you've indicated he knows I went to Eleanor's flat with the police after I left the hospital. That's when I discovered she had cleared out."

Daphne appeared more inclined to believe him.

Douglas spoke with greater emphasis. "I have no idea whether I'll ever hear from her or see her again." That, he realized, also was true.

"I don't envy your marriage," she said, snuggling still closer. "But it really hasn't been much of a marriage, has it?"

She appeared determined to seduce him, but his situation was already too complicated. "I'm seriously thinking of going home."

"Soon?" It was impossible to determine whether her disappointment was feigned or genuine.

Douglas thought it would do no harm to exaggerate a bit. "Either on the late flight tonight or tomorrow. I'm not temperamentally suited to the role of a knight errant, and the longer I neglect my practice the heavier my schedule will be when I get back to New York."

There was a suggestion of malicious triumph in her answering smile, and he guessed she was thinking that Eleanor should have known better than to place complete reliance on a husband she hadn't seen in years and had treated shabbily.

"I told Ian you bear him no grudge and won't try to harm him," she said.

"I never heard of him until a few days ago, and I can't imagine any reason our paths should cross again after I leave Hong Kong," Douglas said. "I won't weep if the Preventive Service corners him and sends him to prison, but I won't lose any sleep, either, if he becomes the biggest and most successful gold smuggler on earth."

Daphne's green eyes narrowed as she studied him.

He caught a glimpse of her real nature, and his flesh crawled. She and MacLeod deserved each other.

"Ordinarily," she said, "I wouldn't dream of speaking for Ian. But I think you honestly want no part of what's happening here. So I can promise you that if you're sincere, if you actually intend to leave Hong Kong in the next twenty-four hours and go back to your own world, Ian won't interfere or try to stop you."

"What you're saying is that if I mind my own business and clear out he and his syndicate will guarantee me a safe-conduct pass."

"I wouldn't have put it quite that way," she said, "but I'll accept your terms on Ian's behalf."

Douglas had offered no agreement, but she was revealing her husband's anxiety to be rid of him. Eleanor had been right when she insisted that his involvement created complications the syndicate would find it difficult to overcome.

"I'm sure you resent threats," she continued, "but I think it only fair to warn you that Ian becomes furious when anyone fails to keep his word. I've seen him lose his sense of perspective and become very nasty. It's the one weakness he can't seem to overcome."

In spite of her language, Douglas knew, her meaning was clear: if he continued to meddle in the syndicate's affairs MacLeod would use any means to be rid of him. But this was not the moment to respond defiantly to the challenge. "We understand each other."

She glanced at her diamond and gold watch. "I had no idea it was so late. I really must run."

He made no attempt to detain her.

"I meant it," she said, "when I told you I'm going to get in touch with you in New York. We owe ourselves a celebration, don't you think?"

Giving him no chance to reply, she grasped the back of his head with one hand to pull him closer, then kissed him. For a moment her lips were soft and passive, then her tongue darted in and out, teasing him, and before he could react she drew away. It was an expert performance, kittenish yet promising intimacy, and even though she didn't achieve her goal of arousing him he had to admire the proficiency of her technique.

Daphne rose, smiled warmly and was gone.

Douglas scrubbed his mouth with a tissue, ordered another drink and downed it in a few swallows. Daphne MacLeod was as evil, perhaps as dangerous, as her husband.

Certainly his own situation had become more precarious as a result of this encounter. By encouraging her to believe he wanted to wash his hands of any involvement in the affairs of the syndicate and by indicating that he intended to leave Hong Kong in the immediate future, he had given her a false picture of his plans.

The real truth was that the syndicate's threats had strengthened his resolve. He had never liked being pushed around, and was damned if a gang of international criminals was going to frighten him so badly that he ran for cover.

Certainly Eleanor's fear of the syndicate was justified, and he couldn't blame her for going into hiding. At least the session with Daphne had solidified his belief that she hadn't been abducted or injured by the gang.

His own uncertainties vanishing, Douglas knew what had to be done. He would wait another twenty-four hours for Eleanor to get in touch with him. If he did not hear from her by that time he would go to Sir Frederick Simpson and volunteer his services in any way he could be used. People like Ian and Daphne MacLeod were menaces to law-abiding, decent people everywhere, and his conscience wouldn't let him rest until they were sent to prison.

XIV

Douglas had no appetite for the dinner he ate in the hotel coffee shop, the evening dragged and his sleep was restless. The early-morning sun slanting in through the blinds awakened him, and he drank more coffee than was good for him as he read the morning newspapers. He was uncertain what he expected to find, but felt let down when he saw no mention of Eleanor's disappearance.

The morning passed slowly, and he returned to the coffee shop for his third successive meal there. His spirits flagging, he was ready to give up hope that Eleanor would try to make contact with him. Perhaps she had decided to escape alone from both the gold syndicate and the Preventive Service, and he couldn't blame her if she went into hiding for a long time to come. If he were in her position he might find it expedient to vanish, too, without telling anyone where he was going.

Suddenly, in midafternoon, the ringing of his telephone broke the long silence.

"Don't mention my name," Eleanor said. "This line may be bugged."

"Okay." Just hearing her voice and knowing she was safe gave him a sense of far greater relief than he would have thought possible. But this was not the moment to express his feelings.

"Can you meet me in five minutes?"

"Sure, but I—"

"Good. You have no idea how popular you are. You're being watched by everybody in town, so you'll have to give them all the slip." In spite of an underlying note of urgency she was unhurried. "Use the service elevator at the end of the corridor and turn left when you reach the ground floor. You'll see the exit, and you'll come out on the street behind the hotel. I'll meet you there in exactly five minutes. Don't be late."

She rang off before he could speak again, and the line went dead.

Douglas was in a quandary. By following her instructions he would escape from the protective surveillance of the Preventive Service agents assigned to guard him. If he tried to alert them, however, he would advertise his departure to the syndicate's operatives and through him they would find Eleanor. Her plan might be faulty, but she had given him no time to consider alternatives, and if he hesitated she might not run the risk of getting in touch with him again.

Hastily donning a lightweight jacket, he started off down the corridor, and not until he drew near the service elevators did it occur to him that he wasn't wearing a necktie. It was too late to go back for one, however, so he pressed the elevator button, and a few moments later a car appeared. It was empty, and his tension dissipated somewhat as he stepped inside.

It halted after descending a few floors, and the Chinese chambermaid who entered, her arms filled with folded towels, glanced at him. A Chinese waiter joined them at another stop, and was equally curious about the foreigner. Seeing the couple repeatedly looking at each other, Douglas expected trouble; at the least they would challenge him, and at the worst they would summon a member of the hotel's security force. Either way there would be a delay, and Eleanor might not wait for him to appear. He pretended to be unaware of the others' surreptitious scrutiny and hoped he looked more at ease than he felt.

The chambermaid left on a lower floor, but the waiter remained in the car until they reached the street level. Douglas, turning to the left, was relieved when the man went off in the opposite direction, and he told himself he would never grow accustomed to a life beyond the confines of the law.

The heat of urban Hong Kong enveloped him as he reached the street, and he began to perspire. Several trucks were parked near the service entrance, one from a bakery and the other bearing the name of a laundry. The usual crowds of pedestrians were everywhere, but he saw no sign of Eleanor.

A small dilapidated sedan pulled to a halt directly in front of Douglas, and when the door on the passenger's side opened he saw a woman in a wide-brimmed hat and large sunglasses behind the wheel.

"Get in," Eleanor said. "We're blocking traffic."

He sat beside her, and she pulled away from the curb before he could close his door.

She looked repeatedly in the rearview mirror, and they rode several blocks before she spoke. "We made it," she said. "I'm fairly certain we're not being followed. Keep watch for me, and let me know if any car seems to be staying behind us."

He did as he was bidden. "What happened to your own car?"

Eleanor's laugh was harsh. "I've been planning this step for a long time. Everybody knows my convertible."

"I was beginning to think I wouldn't hear from you," he said.

"Then you know how I felt yesterday. I emptied the flat, leaving no trace, and I expected you to join me. When you didn't come I was sure you'd deserted me. I didn't learn about poor Ho Fang until last night."

"The syndicate killed him?"

"The direct, personal orders of MacLeod, the bastard. How I'd love to repay him before this caper ends!" She controlled herself with difficulty. "Anyone behind us?"

"No, the traffic pattern keeps changing." He saw she was heading toward the overpass that would take them to the new Kowloon tunnel under the harbor.

"Tell me what's happened to you since yesterday," Eleanor said. "And don't leave out anything."

He told her in detail about his meetings with Chief Inspector Li and Sir Frederick Simpson.

"They're no friends of mine," she said. "And no matter what they told you, they were planning to use you as a stalking horse. They offered you protection in the hope you'd lead them to me."

"At least they won't shoot us on sight, which may be more than I can say for the syndicate." Douglas went on to tell her about his session with Daphne MacLeod.

"That tramp! I'd strangle her if she got you into bed!"

He found her unexpected vehemence flattering, the outburst of jealousy indicating that perhaps she regarded him as something more than the means to her own ends.

Eleanor switched on her headlights as they entered the underwater tunnel. "I'm sorry I've caused you so much grief, Doug. Just have faith in me, that's all, and we'll come out of this in a way that will be great for both of us."

"I can't help wishing," he said, "that we were cooperating with the Preventive Service."

"Never! All they want is to protect their civil service records, and to hell with people. We'd be in worse trouble if we took them at their word!"

If he was any judge, Sir Frederick was reliable as well as honorable, but he couldn't argue with Eleanor, whose hatred of authority seemed pathological. But he couldn't help asking, "Do you think we can handle that bloodthirsty syndicate crew by ourselves?"

"We'll soon find out," she said, and her calm was deceptive. "In another minute or two we'll be leaving the tunnel. I'd like you to take the wheel. Head up onto the cloverleaf, and when you come to a divided highway take the fork on the right. Okay?"

"Sure." He saw her looking into the rearview mirror, her lips compressed.

The sedan shot out of the tunnel into the daylight.

"Now," Eleanor said.

"Aren't you going to stop so we can change places?"

Instead of replying she climbed over him into the passenger's side.

The car began to swerve, and Douglas righted it as he slid behind the wheel.

Eleanor laughed. "Good show! I knew we'd make a first-rate team."

"We could have gone out of control and had a smashup. You should have warned me." He was irritated as he drove onto the cloverleaf.

"No, you'd have found too many sensible objections, and there wasn't time."

Flicking a glance at her, he saw her take her silencer-equipped Lilliput from her shoulder bag and lower the window beside her.

The car behind them was drawing closer, and Douglas looked into the rearview mirror. The vehicle was large, American-made, and was occupied by two men. The passenger reached into a shoulder holster, and Douglas felt a chill when he saw the man drawing a revolver.

"Hold steady," Eleanor said, and pumped a hail of bullets into the other car's front tires.

The driver tried to maintain control, but the odds against him were too great, and the larger car spun in a semicircle before crashing into a concrete-reinforced railing of steel at the side of the cloverleaf.

"Faster!" Eleanor said. "Let's get out of their range."

Douglas pushed the accelerator to the floor, and the old sedan responded instantly, leaping forward so quickly that he barely managed to turn onto the right fork in time. All at once he realized that, in spite of its appearance, this was no ordinary car. "What an engine!"

"It should be."

"And what accurate shooting."

"I'm out of practice," she said, "but I didn't do too badly, did I?"

"Since I've just been a party to something the police would

disapprove," Douglas said, "I think I have a right to know what that was all about."

Under the circumstances her lighthearted giggle seemed incongruous. "They work for Ian and I recognized them, although their car was new. I thought we were clean when we left the hotel, and I have no idea how they picked up our trail. But it doesn't matter now." Again she became brusque. "Leave the highway at this exit, bear left at the underpass and follow the road that runs parallel to it."

In a few moments he found they were on a broad street lined with old-fashioned paving blocks. There were tenements on both sides of the road, some of five or six stories, some two or three times that height, and pushcarts filled every foot along both curbs. The street itself was littered with garbage, and Douglas realized they were driving through a slum district.

"Not so fast," Eleanor said. "There will be real trouble if we hit a pedestrian. This is one part of town where it doesn't pay to be mistaken for an Englishman."

He slowed the sedan to a crawl.

"That's better," she said, and directed him to a parking place on a narrow side street.

He switched off the engine and had to wait while she applied a thick coating of a bright lipstick to her mouth, and when she removed her sunglasses he saw she was wearing heavy eye makeup. He locked the car behind them, and for the first time noticed that she was wearing a *cheongsam* of sleazy material that was a size too small for her.

"You look like a tart," he said.

"I hope so." Eleanor took his arm and, walking close to him, guided him toward a cluster of high-rise tenements. Balconies cluttered with tomato plants and livestock were protected by metal grilles, and made the whole complex resemble a pile of giant bird cages.

"What's the idea?"

"We'll be taken for granted," she said, "only if they think I'm a prostitute and you're my customer. In this neighborhood they know of no other reason for contact between a Chinese and a foreigner."

They reached the first of the ten- to fifteen-story buildings, which were packed so closely together there was no space between them.

On the ground floor of the nearest were establishments that looked like shops, but when Douglas looked through the plate glass windows he saw they were dentists' operating rooms.

Eleanor was aware of his puzzled expression and laughed. "These are refugee dentists from mainland China who work here without Hong Kong licenses. They're among the best in town, and their prices are so reasonable they have more patients than they can handle."

"What is this place?"

"The Kowloon Walled City."

Suddenly he understood. When the British had occupied Hong Kong in the mid-nineteenth century this tract of six and a half acres had been set aside as Chinese territory. The mandarin who lived in nearby Canton had planned to build a palace there, but had never bothered, and the tenements had grown instead. The Walled City, in theory, had belonged to the Nationalist government of Chiang Kai-shek and Mao Tse-tung's Reds, in turn, and the Crown Colony government had been careful not to exercise jurisdiction there.

In practice the settlement was governed by a coalition of local tongs, or gangs, and Douglas was familiar with the place because the Hong Kong newspapers were filled with stories about vicious crimes supposedly committed there. The Hong Kong police, it was said, entered the compound only on rare occasions, and no fewer than six or eight armed men comprised such raiding parties.

Eleanor was watching Douglas, awaiting his reaction.

"Why the Walled City?"

"The Preventive Service and police aren't welcome, and neither is the syndicate. One hundred thousand people live in this tiny area, mostly because the rent is so cheap, and they're encouraged to mind their own business."

"I still don't see—"

"We'll be safe here as long as we want to stay," Eleanor said, "and I'll have a chance to work out some final arrangements. I had to move my whole schedule forward when MacLeod ordered me to go to Manila as a courier, and there are a few loose ends to be tied up."

The idea of going into hiding in one of the world's most crowded, crime-ridden slums did not appeal to Douglas, and he made his distaste plain.

"I did a favor several years ago for one of the Walled City landlords, and these people never forget." An opening between two buildings, a crude entrance only one story high, stood directly ahead, and Eleanor urged him toward it. "All they ask is that we obey their rules, and no one will touch us."

"I can't see why this should be necessary."

"I'll explain after we're inside." She preceded him down a short flight of worn stone steps.

Douglas found himself in the dimly lighted interior of the Walled City, where the buildings literally leaned against each other about two stories above his head. Underfoot was a narrow path of hard-packed dirt, and at one side was a cement trough in which a trickle of dirty water was inching toward the Hong Kong gutter outside.

A slender Chinese appeared out of the gloom, a bulge in his expensive sports shirt revealing the outline of a pistol in a shoulder holster beneath it.

Eleanor addressed him in Cantonese, her tone so low that Douglas could hear only an occasional word.

The security guard nodded from time to time, meanwhile studying the foreigner with infinite care, and Douglas had never seen such open hostility. Finally the girl's explanation appeared to satisfy him, and he waved them ahead.

The path was so narrow they had to walk single file. "Speak to no one," Eleanor murmured. "Touch no one, and pretend you don't see any strange sights you might find offensive. Stay close behind me."

He remained on her heels as they moved deeper into the labyrinth down the winding path. Occasionally they passed the open door of a tiny textile factory, and twice they saw primitive restaurants, where scrawny Chinese in undershirts sat at bare wooden tables, eating bowls of noodles being cooked in large iron pots on single-burner stoves.

Here and there the path grew wider for a few yards, and emaciated men were sleeping on the ground in these openings. Their presence was inexplicable until Douglas saw a line of men waiting patiently outside a closed door. As he and Eleanor walked past it he smelled the pungent, unmistakable odor of burning opium, and all at once the mystery was solved. An illegal divan was located on the far side of the door, catering to men so poverty-stricken that only drug-inspired dreams gave them reason to remain alive.

Sometimes a small child appeared on the path, a reminder that entire families lived in the Walled City. The demeanor of these youngsters was grave, and it occurred to Douglas that he had not heard one person speak since he and Eleanor had left the security guard behind. Perhaps silence was obligatory in public here; certainly the gloom was not conducive to animated conversation.

After a walk that seemed endless Eleanor came to a wooden ladder, its rungs held in place by thongs, and began to climb it.

Douglas followed, and when he had left behind the few dirty windows that cast a feeble light on the ground floor, he was plunged into complete darkness. He could hear Eleanor above him, but could not see her, and for the first time he realized that the heat was suffocating. His clothes were soaked, and sweat dripped from his forehead into his smarting eyes.

"There's a landing on each floor," Eleanor said, "with the ladder beside it. We'll keep climbing."

The ascent seemed endless, and although Douglas tried to count he was uncertain whether they were on the eleventh or twelfth floor when Eleanor made her way down another corridor. Their footsteps creaked, and Douglas wondered whether the floorboards might give way. What astonished him most was that tens of thousands of human beings lived in these dismal surroundings.

Eleanor opened a door, closing and bolting it after Douglas followed her, and he was momentarily blinded by the late-afternoon sunlight streaming in through the bars of a balcony cage, where tomatoes and scallions were growing in a dozen clay pots.

The room itself was about fifteen feet long and ten feet wide, with a straw rug partly covering the floor. A large mattress was the most prominent object in the chamber, the other furniture consisting of a small alcohol-burning stove and a table on which bread, sausages and packages of other foods were piled. Several corked jugs stood on the floor near the table, and a small radio rested on a wall shelf. The breeze that blew in from the balcony was hot, but at least the air was relatively fresh. From the balcony there was a glimpse of the tar-paper roof of a Hong Kong tenement across the street.

A kerosene lamp and two candles rested on a small shelf attached to a bare wall, and Eleanor saw Douglas glance at them.

"Living conditions here are more primitive than on Park Avenue," she said. "There's no electricity or running water in the Walled City, so I've made arrangements for our chamber pots to be picked up."

He continued to look at the lamp and candles. "The fire hazard in this place must be enormous."

"It is," she agreed. "But there has been no major fire since one was set deliberately during the Japanese occupation of Hong Kong in World War Two. People were protesting when they tore down the wall around the compound for paving blocks."

"How do they prevent fires?"

"Everyone is careful." She took the extraordinary self-discipline of the Chinese for granted. "Those who own very little can't afford to lose their few possessions."

Douglas wandered out to the cluttered balcony, then returned to the room. The quarters were so confined it would be difficult to remain here for even a short time.

But it was obvious that Eleanor was pleased with the arrangements she had made. "We have enough food and water for a week," she said, "and I can always buy more if we stay longer. And we can drink rice wine with our dinner."

"A week!" He thought of his crowded waiting room, of the mounting backlog of patients who awaited his return.

"I forgot to get you a razor and some clean clothes, but I'll buy them tomorrow."

"I have a couple of suits at the hotel. And my instruments are there."

"No," she said, and her voice was firm. "The police will be watching your hotel, and so will Ian MacLeod, so you can't go back there. Your belongings will be held for you, and after everything is settled you'll be able to send for them."

"I've been maneuvered into an untenable position," Douglas said. "I feel like a fugitive, and for all practical purposes I'm a prisoner in the Walled City."

"You know too much."

"What I want to know is how long I'll have to hide out in this place!"

"You've learned a great deal about my situation," Eleanor said. "And I'm grateful to you for your help. I intend to prove my gratitude."

He tried to interrupt, but she silenced him with a sharp gesture.

"There are some things I haven't been able to tell you yet. You'll understand my reasons when the right time comes. I married you because I fell in love with you, and I believe you realize I still love you."

She seemed sincere, and he could think of no reason to deny her claim.

"As you'll discover," she said, "I'm fighting for our future, our security. Don't ask questions I can't answer yet. And trust me."

"I wouldn't be here if I didn't."

"There are no lies that stand between us," she said. "And I swear I won't fail you."

He tried to reconcile himself to the prospect of a prolonged stay in this strange place.

"Those who have a choice don't come to the Walled City, Doug, and we're no exception. We won't stay here an hour longer than we must. If things work out as I hope we'll be able to leave in a day. Two days at most."

"That's good to hear."

"Until then we could be in a worse spot. We're safe. We have enough to eat and drink. And we have each other." Unzipping her dress, she removed her clothes and stood before him nude.

XV

Eleanor left the Walled City room at noon to buy Douglas a razor and some clean clothes, and he gathered she also planned to attend to some unexplained matters that would expedite their departure. Alone for the first time since they had come here, he weighed his situation.

They had made love repeatedly since the previous afternoon, strengthening their bond and at the same time increasing his obligation to see her through her crisis. He had no idea how she could manage their escape from both the authorities and the gold syndicate, and it was inconceivable to him that United States immigration officials would admit her to the country without arresting her. But she continued to express the conviction that all would be well, so he was forced to accept her optimistic prediction without knowing her reasons for it. No matter what she said, their position was precarious.

He paced the room for a time, then picked his way to the outer side of the caged balcony. By craning his neck he could catch a glimpse of the heavy slum traffic in the street outside the Walled City, and at eye level was an expanse of tar-paper tenement roofs, each with its own shallow porcelain pool for rain catchment.

Suddenly he remembered the little radio on the wall shelf, and returning hastily to the room, he snapped it on. The batteries still worked, and the sounds of a Beethoven symphony flooded the room. Douglas wanted to preserve the batteries, so he turned the radio off and, after glancing at his watch, waited five minutes for the next local newscast.

The announcer discussed various matters approved by the Governor's Council, then read the Hong Kong stock market report and the latest import-export trade figures. Restless and bored, Douglas debated whether to turn the radio off again, but before he could make up his mind the voice of the announcer became crisp:

"Now for a special report. A prominent American surgeon, Dr. Douglas Gordon, has disappeared from his fashionable hotel on Hong Kong side. The hotel management says he has not been seen since yesterday afternoon. All of his personal belongings were left behind, so it appears that he intended to return. The United States Consulate General has no information regarding Dr. Gordon's whereabouts.

"Chief Inspector Li of the Hong Kong police is conducting a personal investigation. His office states that no information has yet been received to indicate that Dr. Gordon was abducted for ransom or was the victim of other foul play.

"According to a persistent rumor that neither Radio and Rediffusion nor the newspapers can verify, Dr. Gordon is married to a Hong Kong woman whom the Preventive Service is seeking for questioning about the activities of a gold-smuggling ring with which she is believed to have been connected. A spokesman for the Preventive Service is following the department's usual policy and refuses comment. He will not state, either, whether Dr. Gordon is also on the Preventive Service wanted list.

"The police have offered a reward of five thousand Hong Kong dollars for any information that will make it possible for them to find Dr. Gordon."

The announcer paused, then went on to another subject.

Douglas turned off the radio and felt queasy. Sir Frederick Simpson and Inspector Li were demonstrating their cleverness. Realizing that he had escaped from the surveillance of the plainclothesmen assigned to watch him, they had released just enough information about him to capture the imagination and interest of local citizens. And by coupling that data with the offer of a reward they were improving their chances of locating him.

Even worse was the realization that American newspaper correspondents in the Crown Colony were certain to pick up the story and put it on the cables to their home offices. Before the day ended his name—and the innuendos about him—were certain to appear on the front pages in New York. Douglas shuddered and refused to let himself dwell on the reactions of his patients when they read the accounts.

He wanted to send an immediate cable to Eddie Baker saying he was alive, in good health and that the rumors about him were distorted half-truths. With the authorities alerted, however, he could neither send a cable nor make an overseas telephone call to Eddie. He was helpless unless Eleanor changed her mind and decided to cooperate with Sir Frederick. Meantime his reputation was suffering at home.

His ferment became even more intense, and he was tempted to leave the Walled City and go straight to the nearest telephone, but the knowledge that he might compromise Eleanor's questionable security held him back. When she returned he would insist she tell him her plans, and then he would make his own decisions.

The agony of waiting seemed endless, but at last he heard five taps at the door, their prearranged signal, and slid back the bolt.

A heavily laden Eleanor deposited several bundles on the mattress. "I don't know how I managed to carry all these packages up the ladder."

Douglas closed and bolted the door. "We have some things to settle," he said, "right now."

She saw his expression. "You know," she said, and handed him the afternoon newspapers.

His likeness stared at him from the front pages, and he wondered where the newspapers had obtained his photograph. Then he recognized his necktie and jacket, and remembered he had worn them on his first visit to Preventive Service headquarters. Professional law enforcement officials missed no angles.

"I should have warned you that Sir Frederick would pull some sort of stunt," Eleanor said. "But I couldn't predict exactly what he'd do, so I decided not to worry you in advance. Perhaps you'll believe me now when I tell you he isn't reliable."

"To hell with Sir Frederick! I'm concerned about my good name at home."

"Of course you are, but we're going to act so quickly that no real harm will be done. Here, you'll want to shave and change, and then we'll be leaving. Much sooner than I had thought."

He poured water into a basin and became busy with shaving soap and razor. "I want to know what's ahead. Spell it out for me."

"By midnight we'll be far from Hong Kong," she said as she changed her own clothes.

"I realize that neither the Preventive Service nor MacLeod's people know where to look for us. But Kaitak Airport must be crawling with agents who are carrying our descriptions."

"Give me credit for a little sense, darling. We aren't going near the airport."

"I'm sure the authorities and the syndicate must be watching the waterfront, too. The only other way out of Hong Kong is by train to Canton. The Chinese wouldn't admit me, and you can't be anxious to go there, either."

"Oh, they'd admit us. Think of the fun they'd have making us the principals in a spy trial."

"Well, then?"

"Far more than gold has been smuggled out of Hong Kong," Eleanor said.

"By ship, you mean."

"Yes, the deal is set. Does that satisfy you?"

"Not really." He finished shaving, glanced at her and stopped short. She had removed her makeup, a loose shirt and pants of dark cotton concealed her figure and her entire appearance was altered.

"Surprise," she said. "Disguises are dangerous, and simple methods are the most effective. Very few people who know me would recognize me now." She handed him several bundles. "It's your turn."

He examined nondescript trousers, shirt and rubber-soled shoes, but grimaced at the sight of a long-sleeved workingman's jacket.

"It's too hot for this."

"You'll need it," she said, unpacking a shoulder holster and .32-caliber pistol, which she calmly proceeded to load. "You can't walk around in public wearing firearms."

Douglas blinked and was speechless.

"Please change, darling. We don't want to waste any time, and every hour is important."

"I've never carried a gun. And I haven't fired one since the U. S. Army gave me a special practice course before I was sent to Vietnam. So I can't—"

"The syndicate's men are armed. So are the police and the Preventive Service agents. Why should you be at a disadvantage?"

"Damn it, I'm a surgeon, not a gunman!"

Eleanor slid the holster strap over his shoulder and buckled it into place. "I hope you'll have no need to use it, but you might find it comforting in an emergency," she said, dropping a packet of spare bullets into his jacket pocket.

Her logic was irrefutable, so he took the pistol, balanced it in the palm of his hand and then placed it in the holster.

"One last touch," Eleanor said, giving him a pair of tinted steel-rimmed glasses.

Douglas looked at his reflection in the room's only mirror, and had to admit he more closely resembled a laborer than a Park Avenue surgeon. Most of his patients would look hard at him before they recognized him. "Now what?"

"I've already paid a fee to the people from whom I borrowed this place, but they'll appreciate the gift of the clothes and food we leave behind. They've never had such a windfall."

He realized she had made it impossible for him to insist on taking his belongings with them.

She glanced around the room, her expression wistful. "I'll remember this place. We've been here less than twenty-four hours, but we've been happy."

On sudden impulse he kissed her.

She clung to him, then moved away and started toward the door. "Let's go." Her voice had a metallic ring.

He towered above her on the long climb to the ground floor, taking his time on the ladder so he wouldn't step on her hands, and at last they reached the gray half-light of the winding path.

"We don't look the way we did when we came here," Eleanor

murmured. "If we're stopped, let me handle things. No matter what might happen, don't start a fight."

They walked single file down the hard dirt path, and Douglas sensed a greater hostility in the people they encountered. He and Eleanor no longer looked like a local prostitute and her Western client, and the Chinese inhabitants of the Walled City openly resented the presence of outsiders who didn't belong there.

The American was relieved when he caught a glimpse of bright sunlight ahead, but he checked himself when a security guard appeared and blocked the path. Eleanor spoke to him at length in Cantonese, but he shook his head, and when he whistled softly a second guard joined him.

Douglas braced himself for trouble, but Eleanor warned with a glance not to interfere.

The second guard appeared to be a man of greater authority, and she addressed herself to him.

He, too, was dissatisfied, and issued a curt command.

"They want to search us," Eleanor said, raising her hands over her head.

The senior guard frisked her first, taking his time and obviously enjoying himself as he ran his hands up and down her body.

Her face was wooden, her eyes blank.

Douglas felt a sudden surge of jealousy. His wife was being humiliated by this stranger who was pawing her, and he clenched his fists. Suddenly, however, he realized the other guard was watching him with a sardonic grin, waiting for an excuse to attack him. It was difficult to obey Eleanor's injunction not to start something, but he forced himself to subside.

Then it was his turn, and rough hands patted him. He was surprised when the guard paid no attention to the pistol under his jacket, and soon the ordeal was ended.

Eleanor waited at the steps that led to the Hong Kong street. "They thought we might be trying to smuggle out drugs," she said.

"Smuggle them *out?*"

"Of course. The Walled City overlords want addicts to come there for drugs, and I've been told the Preventive Service likes it that way, too. They can keep a closer watch on the divans instead of searching all over town for new ones."

Douglas realized he would never understand the ways of the East. "I didn't like his groping."

"Both of them knew you were spoiling for a fight, and were just waiting to cut you down. They thought you were English, so they'd have done anything to make you lose face. They like to think of themselves as patriots, even though they'd be sent to prison as parasites if the Reds took over. We'll walk in the center of the street, where there's less garbage."

"We're heading away from the place where we parked yesterday," Douglas said.

"Of course. That car lost its usefulness when we stopped the pair who were following us. By now Ian has passed along a full description to every member of his organization." She turned at the corner and headed up a broad street lined with open-fronted shops.

"What now?"

She halted, smiling as she pointed to a sign overhead.

He was astonished to see they were standing at a bus stop.

"What better way to travel is there for those who want to be inconspicuous?" Eleanor asked, and laughed.

The life she had led had made her shrewd, he thought. No members of the upper and middle classes—Chinese, English or foreign—ever set foot on a Hong Kong bus. It was unlikely that either MacLeod or the authorities would think of setting up a watch on the major bus routes.

After a short wait they climbed aboard a lumbering vehicle as it ground to a halt, and sat side by side. Eleanor was careful to have no physical contact with Douglas and stared straight ahead, as though they were either strangers or barely knew each other.

He quickly understood the reason for her caution. The other passengers, all of them shabbily clad Chinese, stared at them with a curiosity mixed with the same hostility they had encountered in the Walled City. On the surface Hong Kong might be a satisfied British Crown Colony, but a deep-rooted ferment was at work, and Douglas felt uncomfortable.

They spent almost a half hour on the bus, leaving at the last stop, near the Star Ferry, which carried passengers across the harbor, and for the first time Eleanor drew closer. "This is the only time we'll be in danger," she said. "Stay near to me."

Douglas nodded, realizing they were caught up in heavy pedestrian traffic as office workers and shop employees headed back to work after their lunch hour.

Eleanor increased her pace, and seemed to be heading toward

Nathan Road, but shortly before reaching it she darted into a narrow alleyway and broke into a run.

Uncertain whether they were being followed, he glanced back over his shoulder as he remained close behind her, but he could see no one.

At the far end of the alleyway the girl halted beside a nondescript delivery truck. A key was already in her hand, and she unlocked the door. "It will look better if you drive," she said. "Get behind the wheel. Quickly."

He slid into the driver's seat.

Eleanor relaxed beside him and lighted a cigarette. "We'll be all right now," she said.

"Were we spotted?"

"Not to my knowledge, but I wanted to cut down the possible chances."

A police siren sounded in the distance, and drew closer.

She reached into her shoulder bag for her Lilliput, then changed her mind. "A gun battle would do us no good here," she said. "They could seal off both ends of the alley."

For a moment, he realized, she had actually planned to fight rather than surrender, and he knew she was even more determined to escape than he had thought.

The siren drew still closer, then began to fade.

Eleanor opened the window beside her and flicked ashes onto the cobblestones. "I hate being trapped in a place like this. Let's get out."

He turned on the ignition, and the touch of his foot on the gas pedal told him what he suspected: the truck, like the car they had used the previous day, was far more powerful than it appeared.

"You'll have to turn right here," she said. "Head into Kowloon."

"Where are we going?"

"I'll give you directions."

Douglas knew she had deliberately misunderstood his question and had no intention of revealing their destination. Her extreme caution was irritating, and he wondered if there were aspects of their situation he hadn't been told. "This truck," he said, "has a fancy engine."

"It should."

"So did the car we drove yesterday."

She nodded.

"Where do you pick up these super-specials?"

"In Hong Kong," she said, "anything is available for money, and the sellers aren't inquisitive."

"Meaning that I am," Douglas said. "But the difference is that they aren't sticking their necks out. I am."

She apologized by putting her hand on his arm for a moment and applying gentle pressure, but her determination to tell him no more than necessary was unaltered.

"A final question—for now." He gestured toward the rear. "What are we carrying?"

"Nothing. There are a few empty boxes and oil drums in the back, and a greasy tarpaulin or two, I believe. I just bought it today, and I've had no time to inspect it, but I'm sure it contains nothing of value. The man who sold it to me is no philanthropist."

They edged forward in heavy traffic, stopping every few feet.

She donned her oversized sunglasses and handed him a pair larger than the tinted spectacles he was wearing.

He raised an eyebrow.

"We'll be that much harder to recognize. And ordinary people—drivers and pedestrians, too—will pay less attention to us."

"You think of everything," Douglas said.

"I've thought of little else for years," Eleanor said, and smiled. "But the waiting and the planning have been worth my while. Because my dreams are finally being realized and you're sharing them with me."

XVI

Industrial plants, factories and warehouses extended toward infinity on both sides of the wide thoroughfare, which was choked with trailer trucks, and other plants formed a wide belt that began in Kowloon and inched into what had been New Territories farmlands when Douglas last visited Hong Kong six years earlier. Most of the buildings were only a few stories high, but clusters of high-rise apartment houses stood on side streets. Their presence was a tribute to the city planners, who had made certain that workers would be able to live within walking distance of their jobs.

The few trees that stood on either side of the street were fighting a losing battle with air pollution, the afternoon sun was scorching and Douglas drove the little truck at a snail's pace, halting every few yards and waiting interminably before he could start again. He was perspiring heavily, but Eleanor looked cool and unruffled, her manner serene, and he became increasingly irritated.

"There must be a quicker way to leave Hong Kong," he said.

"We aren't going until tonight. It will be so much easier to move from one place to another after dark."

"What are we doing in the meantime—going for a joyride to kill the afternoon?"

"I have a very important appointment," she said. "Our whole financial future depends on it."

"I earn enough to support us, so I don't care if you leave without a penny."

"I care," Eleanor said. "I've worked hard for many years to earn a large sum, even by your American standards, and I have no intention of losing it."

Douglas was surprised by the hard finality of her tone. After their separation he had wondered whether she was greedy, and the thought occurred to him again. Of course she was entitled to her earnings, although the authorities might dispute their legality, and he couldn't blame her for not wanting to give up what she claimed was a tidy amount. Perhaps he was being too sensitive, but it was her attitude that troubled him. Whenever the subject of her finances arose her whole character was altered; her femininity seemed to drain away, and she became harsh, reminding him of the joyless gamblers he had seen years earlier in the Macao casino.

He was eager to give her the benefit of every doubt, however, and tried again. "Since we're partners in every sense now, and I've increased my own risks, it strikes me I have a right to know something about this business of yours."

She was silent for a long time. "You do," she said at last, and chose her words with care. "I own an interest in Ian's syndicate."

He was surprised, having regarded her as an employee.

"A relatively small interest when you consider the enormous profits he and his bosses make. But it's enough to buy an estate in Central America or Brazil and spend most of my time there until we can straighten out my situation with the American immigration officials."

It wasn't too late for her to backtrack, he thought, and cooperate with the Preventive Service. If she did it would be far easier to persuade the U. S. Government to drop any charges against her that might be pending. But this was not the right moment to mention the possibility. He was learning something, and didn't want her to become wary and evasive again.

"Who is your customer?" he asked.

"One of the very top men in another syndicate."

"You're going to meet him?"

"Yes, and so are you, darling. This afternoon."

"Isn't that dangerous?"

Eleanor laughed. "I'll be safer under his roof than I've been for a long time. The managing partners of a syndicate are men of breeding. It would be beneath them to resort to violence or to permit their underlings to use force when one is dealing with them. Their standards are as high as those of your profession."

He smothered a grin and decided he wanted to meet this gold-smuggling paragon. "Will the MacLeod syndicate be willing to accept a competitor as a partner?"

"They have no voice in what I do," she said, and afraid she was revealing too much, she became cryptic. "Besides, it isn't that kind of a deal."

He realized he had to curb his curiosity a little longer. There were fewer factories on the street now, traffic was growing thinner and he was able to increase his speed, holding the truck at thirty miles per hour. There were no plants or apartment houses ahead, no clusters of open-fronted shops, and the pedestrians vanished. The road gave the illusion of growing narrower, although it was the same width, because there were no sidewalks, either.

With startling abruptness the industrial area came to an end and the truck rolled into the New Territories that Douglas recalled so vividly, a region of small farms and rice paddies, tiny cottages and ancient temples. This was the China that had existed for thousands of years, long before the time of the Greek and Roman empires, when the Americas had been populated by savages.

Various shades of green predominated, and all were brilliant, from the pale but intense green of Chinese cabbages to the deeper hues of buckchoy and beans. Bamboo grew wild in patches at the side of the road, and was used principally for fencing that marked property boundaries.

Women of all ages in black pajamas and conical broad-brimmed hats toiled in the fields and waded through the rice paddies, unmindful of the sun and heat. Horned water buffalo pulled curved plows of wood, and were guided by men who had no idea their work was done by modern machines in other lands. Small solemn children in school uniforms similar to those seen in the British Isles walked single file at the side of the road, niether pausing nor even glancing at the truck and its occupants. In the distance temple bells tinkled faintly, but the toilers and children alike ignored their sweet sound. In the New Territories countryside the calendar had been turned back hundreds of years.

At Eleanor's direction Douglas took the sea road that ran the length of a U-shaped bay. In every inlet and cove stood a tiny fishing hamlet that had existed for centuries, and on the far side of the bay, nestled below ancient hills, were identical villages on the soil of Red China. Sampans from both sides of the border met in the bay, and men of both nationalities dredged the bottom for shellfish, using techniques that had been familiar to their common ancestors. Urban Hong Kong seemed far away, as remote as Canton, the southernmost city of China, to which thousands of Crown Colony residents traveled each year to visit relatives.

Only a few miles from the border the truck headed inland again, and Eleanor indicated their destination, a village of about a hundred one-room stone houses, laid out in neat rows and surrounded by a high stone wall. There were a number of these villages in the New Territories, and although the inhabitants had no need for protection from coastal pirates, they neither tore down the walls nor enlarged their communities.

Douglas parked a short distance from an open iron gate, where two men slumped in primitive bamboo chairs were dozing in the sun.

"We'll leave our guns in the truck," Eleanor said, "and don't lock it. They'd be insulted if they thought we didn't respect their honesty."

As they walked toward the gate, where a mongrel dog was stretched at the feet of one of the men, Douglas felt as though he were stepping backward in time. But the walled village was not as removed from the modern world as he had imagined, and he grinned when he saw a television antenna rising from the roof of virtually every hut.

First impressions were deceptive. The men were not sleeping, and watched the approaching couple through narrowed eyes. The dog was alert, too, ready to leap at the intruders if given the command. Douglas noted that both of the sentries were armed with .45 automatics.

But Eleanor was known here, and her arrival created no stir. She exchanged dignified nods with the men, vouching for Douglas with a gesture, and one of the men waved the pair through the gate.

The girl demonstrated her familiarity with the place by heading down a lane toward the far end of the village. The younger men had not yet returned from their day's fishing and the younger women were still at work in the fields, so only the elderly were on hand, some napping on door stoops, others quietly exchanging gossip through the open windows of their huts.

Without exception the residents ignored the new arrivals, showing no curiosity. Douglas observed that they did not bother to glance in the direction of the outsiders, who might as well have been invisible. This lack of interest, although apparently not forced, was unnatural, indicating that this was no ordinary village.

Eleanor slowed her pace as she drew closer to a house two or three times the size of the others. A pajama-clad sentry was lounging against the door, seemingly asleep on his feet, but he roused himself sufficiently to vanish inside the building, and the girl paused at the entrance.

The man returned, waving her in.

Douglas, following close behind her, was surprised to find himself in a modern, handsomely furnished room with a carpeted floor, several comfortable divans and chairs, and indirect lighting.

An inner door opened, and a plump, immaculately groomed Chinese of about sixty in a tailored Western suit came into the room. His calfskin shoes were polished, his nails were manicured and on his left hand he wore a gold and ruby ring that matched his oversized cuff links.

He bowed to Eleanor, addressing her in a harsh Chinese dialect that was unfamiliar to Douglas.

"I have not mastered the tongue of the Chiu Chow," she said. "May we speak in English?"

"Of course. Please accept my apologies, Mrs. Gordon." The man spoke a faultless English.

Douglas looked at him with even greater interest. The Chiu Chow were masters of the Burma-Thailand opium Golden Triangle, and as Sir Frederick had indicated, their overlords were also involved in one of the gold-smuggling syndicates. The trip to this remote spot began to make sense.

"Mr. Wing, permit me to present my husband."

"It is a pleasure to welcome you to my Hong Kong headquarters, Dr. Gordon." The man's handshake, a Western custom he obviously disliked, was flabby. "I have been following your activities in recent days with great interest."

"I seem to have attracted a larger audience than I realized, Mr. Wing," Douglas said.

The Chinese invited them to sit, and an old woman appeared with lacquered cups of a strong, aromatic green tea.

The trio sipped in silence, which Eleanor waited for the host to break.

Wing inspected the scene painted on an ornamental screen, looking at it as though seeing it for the first time. At last he spoke in a low tone. "You weren't followed here?"

"No," Eleanor said. "I checked constantly, and I believe we gave them the slip."

"Don't be too confident, Mrs. Gordon. Ian MacLeod has great competence. I wish I had a few lieutenants endowed with his talents."

This, Douglas thought, had to be one of the Chiu Chow leaders, and it was strange that such a soft, inoffensive man should be one of the most universally feared warlords in the Orient.

"I never underestimate Ian," Eleanor said. "I learned, long ago, that those who do regret it."

Wing nodded. "Very wise. Mind you, Mrs. Gordon, I find it unlikely—inconceivable, really—that MacLeod is unaware of our association. I'm sure he's infiltrated our organization sufficiently to know what we're doing, just as we have people who report to us on what he does."

"Oh, Ian keeps informed. There's no doubt of that." Eleanor seemed unconcerned.

"He'll take no untoward action while you're dealing directly with me or my subordinates," Wing said. "Our unwritten gentlemen's agreement has been effective for many years, and he's no more anxious to start a war than we are. Everyone would lose, and no one would gain."

"I've been counting on Ian's good sense," she said.

"All the same, you won't be completely under our protection before our bargain is consummated, much less later. I've given strict orders that we're not to interfere at such times. I regret the need to show an obvious lack of gallantry, but my colleagues and I have no intention of becoming involved in a costly feud with our competitors."

"I appreciate your position, Mr. Wing, and I wouldn't dream of trying to take advantage of you."

The Chinese bowed. "Just so we understand each other, Mrs. Gordon."

"Perfectly. I assume all risks, but I'm convinced they're diminishing."

The elderly man glanced at Douglas. "I wish you the best of good fortune, too, Dr. Gordon."

The man's eyes were cold, Douglas saw, completely impersonal.

"I haven't bothered my husband with the details of our transaction," Eleanor said.

Wing shrugged as he turned back to her. "As you wish. You're prepared to close our bargain?"

"Right now."

"In daylight?"

"I want to sail as soon after nightfall as possible."

"Very well. You'll need the assistance of two men, I believe you told me."

Eleanor's calm matched Wing's. "If you please."

The Chinese picked up a telephone, pressed a button and spoke into the instrument in such a soft voice that Douglas could not hear a word.

Eleanor stood as soon as the call was completed. "I assume that the arrangements at your end are made."

"You'll find we're as efficient as MacLeod," Wing said. "If there's an accident it won't be due to a failure in either planning or execution on our part."

She inclined her head.

"I'll say good-bye to you, Mrs. Gordon. And to you, Doctor. I'd like to chat with you about the work being done by my nephew, who is a graduate of the Harvard Medical School, but I find it necessary to leave Hong Kong at once. In my position one can't afford to take undue chances." He bowed again, turned and walked through the inner door.

Douglas followed Eleanor back into the open. "What was that all about?"

She walked quickly toward the iron gate, her unexpectedly high-pitched laugh the first sign of nervousness she had betrayed. "I've just made a bargain with a very wealthy and powerful man. So my dreams *will* come true, as you'll soon see."

A sports car was pulling to a stop near the battered truck, and the two burly Chinese in it noted the approach of the couple with blank faces.

Douglas grew taut.

Eleanor placed a reassuring hand on his arm. "They work for Mr. Wing," she said. "They know what must be done, so pay no attention to them."

XVII

The sports car fell in behind the little truck, never allowing more than a few feet of space to intervene between them as Douglas, following Eleanor's instructions, headed up into the hills behind the New Territories seacoast. They drove from one narrow dirt road to another, sometimes doubling back, sometimes taking the same route twice, and the journey seemed endless.

"Another joyride?" Douglas asked.

"I'm making certain we aren't being followed, that's all. Not that we could throw anyone off our trail, but sometimes we reach clearings that let me see all of the approaches below us. A couple of times I've seen other traffic, and I want to be positive in my own mind that Ian's syndicate isn't keeping tabs on us."

"How positive are you?"

"Reasonably, but I don't want to go on to our next stop until the last doubts are gone. We've started the most ticklish phase of my operation, darling, and I can't afford risks now. But I'll do the worrying for both of us."

"You'll have to," Douglas said, "because I haven't any idea what you're doing."

"Trust me a little longer, and you'll have no cause to regret it as long as we live," Eleanor said.

"Okay, but those two behind us have an addiction for tailgate riding, and if I've got to stop short they'll plow into us."

"Never fear, they can take care of themselves."

He had learned better than to persist, and knew it would be a waste of breath to ask the nature of her agreement with the Chiu Chow leader.

Eleanor leaned back against the imitation leather seat of the truck cab. "You're going to be proud of me before the end of the day, Doug. Even Wing Ah was impressed. He isn't usually that polite to people he regards as inferiors. I'm sure he'd have given me a good job in his organization if I'd asked for it."

"Why didn't you?"

"Because I have other plans. I'm going to settle down and spend the rest of my life with my husband. No more capers, no more complications and no more syndicates."

The prospect sounded almost too good to be true, but Douglas could not allow himself to look that far ahead. "We're coming to a fork."

"Take the upper road and go very slowly. We're almost there."

The lane became so narrow and rutted that her advice was superfluous. The truck farms of the New Territories were behind them, and when they reached high ground, about one thousand feet above sea level, they entered a forest of pine and subtropical hardwood trees. The sun could not penetrate here, and the temperature dropped appreciably.

There were no car tracks in the bumpy road, and Douglas crawled forward, the truck protesting as it struggled over uneven pits. The occupants of the sports car, he saw in his rearview mirror, were being jounced even more severely.

Eleanor pointed to a huge banyan tree whose branches formed a bower over the road. "In exactly one mile we'll stop," she said, and her eyes grew bright.

The woods were extensive, and as nearly as he could tell, there were no homes or other buildings in the area.

"Squeeze off the road," Eleanor said, "and park as close to that fir as you can."

Douglas obeyed, and as he halted he realized the sports car had come to a stop behind them.

Eleanor took her Lilliput from her shoulder bag as she climbed to the ground, indicating with a gesture that she thought he should be armed, too.

He disliked the idea, but pocketed the .32 pistol she had provided for him.

Paying no attention to Wing's men, who fell in behind them, she made her way down a path that led to a ravine.

One of the burly Chinese, Douglas saw, was carrying a movers' dolly of thick wood.

They came to a huge metal pipe, which was about six feet in diameter, and walked single file beside it to the lip of the ravine. It disappeared in the underbrush below, then emerged again at the far side.

"This is the water pipe from Red China," Eleanor said.

Douglas was blank.

"The Crown Colony no longer depends on rain water. China sells us hundreds of millions of gallons a year, along with all the meat and rice and vegetables we can't raise ourselves. We survive, and they get the foreign currency they need. Also, we become more dependent on them, which they'd find useful if they should want to force the British out of Hong Kong someday."

She seemed to be making conversation for its own sake, but she had halted now, and began to measure the distance between the metal pipe and a large pine. She took her time, finally marked a spot and then repeated the whole procedure, smiling when her calculations brought her to the same place.

For the first time she and the pair from the sports car communicated. The men glanced at her, and she nodded, pointing with her toe.

The shorter of the men, Douglas saw, was carrying two shovels, and handing one to his companion, he began to dig.

Eleanor took her ease and lighted a cigarette as she leaned against the water pipe to watch.

Douglas joined her, and although the two men dug steadily for more than a half hour they did not find what they were seeking. Ultimately, however, one of them grunted and pointed into the hole.

Eleanor did not stir, and although she missed no move the men made her face betrayed no emotion.

One of the pair jumped into the pit and lashed a nylon rope to an object inside. When he was satisfied that the line was secure he rejoined his companion and they worked in tandem, hauling on the rope until the blood vessels stood out on their foreheads and their muscles bulged, showing through the thin fabric of their shirts.

Just watching them made Douglas weary, but when he started forward to help Eleanor shook her head.

"No," she murmured, "you'd lose face."

The social structure of the East, he thought, was beyond his comprehension.

Another half hour passed before the men succeeded in hauling a small hardwood keg to the surface. It was no more than eighteen inches in diameter, its shell strengthened by thin horizontal bands of metal that had not tarnished underground.

Douglas felt as though he had suffered an electric shock as he stared at the keg. It was so heavy for its size that it could contain only metal, and he knew it had to be filled with gold. At the current legitimate market price, he calculated roughly, it was worth at least one third of a million American dollars, perhaps a great deal more, and would bring double that sum on the underground.

Eleanor saw he knew, but refrained from comment.

The two men managed to hoist the keg onto the dolly and tied it around the planks of wood. Then, after carefully filling in the hole they had dug, they began to haul the cargo in the direction of the waiting vehicles.

Douglas walked with Eleanor behind the dolly, and the short journey seemed endless. The sun was sinking behind the trees by the time they reached the road, and a cooling breeze swept in from the sea.

The two men needed another quarter of an hour to lift the keg into the rear of the truck, which they closed after tying it in place on the floor.

Eleanor moved forward and locked the rear door of the truck.

The two men returned to their sports car and drove off in the direction from which they had come, neither they nor the girl speaking.

At last Eleanor stirred. "We can go now," she said. "We'll stay on this same road. It goes sharply uphill for about half a mile, and soon after we reach the summit the woods will end."

Douglas realized night was falling, and switched on the truck lights before maneuvering back onto the road. "I've read about buried treasure," he said, "but this is the first time I've seen one."

"It belongs to me." Eleanor's voice was uncompromising.

"Isn't it a trifle heavy to take out of the country?" He refrained from mentioning that she would be breaking the law if she failed to secure an export license for the gold.

"I'm selling it to Wing Ah," she said. "He sent two of his men to dig it up for me because I couldn't handle it myself. That was part of the bargain."

The Chiu Chow's syndicate also had arranged her transportation from Hong Kong, Douglas thought, and the outline of her whole plan became clear to him.

Eleanor let the Lilliput rest beside her on the seat, but continued to hold it. "After we reach the crest," she said, "we'll start down the far side and then double back to the sea on a lower road." She glanced at her watch and smiled. "We're doing well, Doug. We're almost a half hour ahead of my schedule."

"Why didn't you turn the keg over to Wing's people where they first found it?" he asked.

She shook her head at his ingenuousness. "Because too many things could have gone wrong before the last step, darling. They could have knocked us out after paying me for the keg and taken the money back. What recourse would I have? Or there might have been a last-minute snag in getting us out of Hong Kong. Wing could always claim that he had no control over what happened, and I'd be out my end of the bargain. No, I refuse to take chances when there's this much at stake."

"How much is that?"

Before she could reply they saw a log that had been thrown across the road, blocking it, and Douglas was forced to bring the truck to a halt.

"Turn off your headlights!" Eleanor directed, and crouched lower in the seat.

He needed no urging before he, too, slid lower.

There was no sign of life on the road ahead or in the clusters of pines at either side.

Eleanor gripped her Lilliput in one hand and with the other cautiously lowered her window a few inches.

It was impossible for Douglas to tell whether the log had fallen across the road or had been placed there.

She nudged him, and he saw a figure stir in the shadows at one side of the road. A moment later someone on the far side inched closer to the clearing.

Douglas' last doubt vanished: MacLeod's men had set an ambush.

A voice with a strong German accent cut through the blanket of gathering night. "We know you're there, Chang!"

Eleanor drew in her breath. "Is that you, Schleiger?"

"It is. Dorfman is with me, and you know we don't play games."

"They're killers," she whispered.

Douglas reluctantly drew the .32 from his pocket.

"Chang," the man called, "I bring you a generous offer from Herr MacLeod. You know what we want, and *we* know you carry it now in the truck. Give it to us, and no harm will come to you and the gentleman."

"Don't believe a word, Doug," Eleanor murmured. "When Ian wants to negotiate he doesn't send these two."

"We're in no position to refuse them," Douglas said. "There isn't room enough to turn the truck around, and we'd be perfect targets if we tried. And I'm afraid we'd break the axle if we bump over that log."

"We aren't beaten yet," she said. "I need a minute or two to think."

The truck's engine continued to idle almost silently.

No one spoke, and the quiet became oppressive.

"Well, Chang?" Schleiger called. "Do you accept or are we going to have trouble?"

"I'm not sure I can trust you." If Eleanor was nervous nothing in her manner or voice betrayed her.

"What guarantees do you want? I give them to you."

"I'm wondering," she replied, "if we can talk about percentages. I'm in a bad spot, so maybe I'm willing to give MacLeod a major share, but I hate to be left in the cold. Are you willing to discuss the angles, Schleiger?"

"Sure." The German spoke too quickly.

"Okay," Eleanor said. "If you'll come into the open I'll meet you halfway."

Douglas was incredulous.

"This will work out," she told him, "but I'll need your help. As soon as I reach the ground put the truck over that log. You have the only advantage, and we need it. Badly."

He had no idea what she intended, but her instructions made sense. The truck became their most potent weapon.

"We agree," Schleiger called. "You come into the open, and we do the same. We move together."

"Fair enough," she replied, then lowered her voice. "Everything depends on you, Doug. Ian has told them you're harmless, so they don't believe you're capable of playing rough."

"I'm not sure I am," he said, gripping the wheel hard with both hands.

Eleanor opened the car door and slid to the outer edge of the seat.

Douglas saw her remove the safety catch from her Lilliput, and an exchange of gunfire seemed inevitable.

MacLeod's men moved cautiously toward the open, one at each side of the road.

Their tactics were crude, but it would be difficult to counter them. Schleiger, who was short and wiry, had selected Eleanor as his target, while his larger companion inched toward the center of the road in an attempt to force Douglas to step to the ground, too.

"Now," Eleanor said, and jumped.

Douglas pushed the gas pedal to the floor, and the truck leaped forward, the door on the passenger's side slamming. He crouched as low as he could, realizing that the startled Dorfman had raised his pistol.

There was a flash, followed by a loud report, and at almost the same instant the upper part of the windshield splintered, a spider's web of cracks spreading across the glass.

Douglas scarcely realized that the shot had passed harmlessly over his head, missing him by inches. He was bearing down on the gunman as the truck gained speed, and all he knew was that he had to kill or be killed.

Dorfman had no chance to fire again.

For a brief moment his terrified face seemed to fill the windshield, and then he disappeared, his hoarse scream rising above the roar of the engine.

Neither then nor later could Douglas determine precisely when he ran the man down. The impact of the front wheels striking and hurtling the log followed so quickly and the jolt was so severe that the two sensations blended into one. Then the rear wheels hit the log and rolled over it.

Douglas found himself on the far side of the barrier, with the truck apparently intact and a clear road ahead. He slammed on the brakes, sickened by the realization that he, who had dedicated himself to the alleviation of suffering, had just taken a human life.

But he resisted the impulse to bury his face in his hands. His own role in the drama had occupied him completely, and he had no idea how Eleanor had fared in her duel with Schleiger. He could see in the rearview mirror that only one figure was standing at the side of the road, and he took a firm grip on the .32 as he climbed out of the truck.

Not allowing himself to look at the crumpled body of Dorfman on the far side of the log, he used the body of the truck as a shield, slowly working his way to the rear. Never in his life had he used firearms in anger, but he was ready to shoot Schleiger before the man could aim at him.

Eleanor came toward the truck, her walk casual.

Douglas stepped into the open, so relieved he felt weak.

She lowered her pistol, then ran to him, and they embraced, clinging to each other fiercely, with no need to speak.

At last they stepped apart, and when Douglas would have checked to see if he could minister to either of MacLeod's men Eleanor halted him. "They're gone," she said, and gently pushed him toward the cab of the truck.

When he had seated himself behind the wheel he began to tremble. Now he, too, was a killer.

Eleanor seemed to understand how he felt. "You had no choice, darling, and neither did I."

"How did you—"

"Schleiger and I exchanged shots as I jumped to the ground. I was a moving target and he wasn't. That's what I was counting on to see me through." She handed him a lighted cigarette.

He struggled briefly, then regained his self-control.

"Let's go," Eleanor said. "They didn't use silencers, you know, and the shots are certain to attract attention. I don't think we want to be in the neighborhood when the police arrive."

Douglas needed no further urging, and the truck started forward, its sturdy frame and axle unharmed. "When MacLeod learns what happened to his men he'll put his whole organization on our trail," he said.

"You should give serious thought to the idea of coming to Central America with me," Eleanor said.

"And abandon my practice? How can I?"

"You can't possibly go back to New York until the furor dies down, and that will be a long time. The syndicate doesn't like it when employees are killed. Ian doesn't forget quickly, and neither do some of the others."

Douglas was too confused to think clearly. They emerged from the woods, and from the heights could see the lights in some of the fishing villages that looked out on the calm waters of the South China Sea. Somewhere below a vessel was waiting that would carry them to safety, but security without freedom was an illusion, and he could only tell himself that he, like his wife, had been forced by circumstances to become a fugitive.

If he gave himself up he would be tried for murder, of that much he was certain. Perhaps he would be freed by the court, but the case would create a sensation and his reputation as a medical practitioner would be destroyed. No patient would understand how he had been trapped, forced to kill in order to save his own life. Members of his profession were expected to live responsible lives, and it would be difficult to explain to anyone how he happened to be roaming through the rural areas of the Hong Kong Crown Colony with a gold-smuggling, exotic wife. His adventures were a tabloid editor's dream come true, and he would never live down the notoriety.

Eleanor misinterpreted his silence. "Please don't worry about money, Doug. We could live comfortably for years just on what Mr. Wing is giving me in my deal with him."

Even a few hours earlier Douglas would not have believed he would be forced to contemplate a life of exile in a tropical banana republic where he would be dependent on the charity and good will of his wife.

She knew he was miserable, and jarred him back to the present. "We won't concern ourselves with tomorrow just yet," she said. "Tonight is just beginning."

He tried to adjust to the reality that their dangers were not ended.

"I could pretend we're safe," Eleanor said, "but that wouldn't be fair to you. Ian is too experienced to have put his complete faith in Schleiger and Dorfman. He's always preached that an automatic is worthless unless you carry spare ammunition clips. Obviously he knows about the keg, and he's sure to have developed alternate plans for getting his hands on it."

"What kind of plans?"

"I'll have to work that out. I made one mistake, Doug, years ago, and it's coming back now to haunt me. I thought that Ian MacLeod knew nothing about the keg. But he had no intention of trying to force me to tell him where it was hidden. He's kept watch over me all this time, knowing that eventually I'd dig it up—and save him the trouble. All he's got to do now is step in and take it from me before I can hand it to Wing Ah's people."

The nightmare was endless.

Eleanor straightened. "Feeling sorry for myself won't solve anything. I know my timetable and Ian doesn't. That's my one advantage, and we're going to use it for all it's worth!"

XVIII

In a fishing hamlet so tiny it had no name Eleanor bought a quantity of smoked fish, roasted peas and a handful of litchi nuts. Douglas found a place to park behind a mountain of oyster shells, fifteen feet high, that had not yet been hauled away to make road-surfacing material, and there, hidden from the road, they ate their simple meal.

They exchanged few words. Douglas continued to see the frenzied face of the man he had run down and knew he would never forget the scene. On rare occasions he had lost patients on the operating table, but in time he had been able to put those tragedies out of his mind. This incident was different, however, and he realized he would always have to live with the knowledge that he had committed a deliberate act of murder.

Eleanor was lost in thought, too, devoting herself completely to the urgent task of outwitting Ian MacLeod. She sifted and weighed ideas, first improvising and then refining, but not until she had finished eating and lighted a cigarette did she speak.

"When I first became a courier," she said, "I was taught to play the odds, and I learned never to go on a mission unless they were in my favor. There were some in the syndicate who believed I was lucky because I was never stopped, never caught in South Korea or Manila, the two places that show no compassion toward gold smugglers. But luck had nothing to do with my success. I went to those places only when I knew the most lenient or careless customs men were on duty. There was one inspector in the Philippines who thought I was a Hong Kong travel agent and fell in love with me. I can't tell you how many kilos of gold I ran through his station. My secret, if that's what you want to call it, was knowing what I was doing and recognizing the weaknesses of my opponents."

Douglas knew she was not boasting, but was stating plain facts as she saw them.

"That's why we're going to beat Ian. He's sure to have figured out that we'll be leaving Hong Kong by sea, but he can only guess the rendezvous where I'll close the deal with Wing Ah's people. It could be any one of a half-dozen places, and Ian doesn't have enough reliable men to cover all of them in force. He'll have to make his biggest effort before we put out to sea. He lacks the strength and the information sources of the Preventive Service, and even they can't halt and inspect more than a few of the boats that sail in and out of Hong Kong every day."

Douglas was uncertain whether she was trying to convince him or herself.

"We'll know within the next hour whether I've calculated the odds correctly this time. Shall we go?"

"Wait," Douglas said. "I've had enough surprises in the past couple of days to last the rest of my life. I've killed a man, which makes me a fugitive from justice, and it looks as though I'll have to give up my profession. I have a right to know the next move on the agenda. I'm tired of being spoon-fed, move by move. I want the complete scenario."

Eleanor considered his demand, and finally smiled. "I can't think of you as an amateur any longer, so you're entitled to know. We're going to a harbor on the far side of the New Territories where one of Wing Ah's lieutenants will be waiting for us with a boat. I'll turn the keg over to him, and he'll give us the boat. He'll also pay me for the keg," she added. "In Swiss francs and U.S. dollars, along with a number of negotiable securities I specified. Wing keeps his word. I keep my word. So it should be a very simple transaction."

He thought it probable that she was deliberately refraining from mentioning the risks they would run, but she didn't know, any more than he did, what specific countersteps MacLeod might be taking. By this time the authorities probably had found the bodies of the two syndicate thugs on the road that ran through the woods, and it was likely that, if the pair had been identified, the police and the Preventive Service might be stepping up the pace of their search, too.

Snapping on the ignition and lights, Douglas returned to the road. They drove for more than five minutes before they saw another vehicle, and traffic remained so light that Eleanor suggested they switch to a major highway for the last lap of their journey. Even here relatively few cars and trucks were abroad, but as they came to more heavily populated areas the pedestrian traffic increased.

They had returned to the more familiar Hong Kong world of factories, government-sponsored housing developments and high-rise tenements. Other vehicles appeared in ever-increasing numbers, and as Douglas concentrated on his driving Eleanor kept constant watch to make sure they weren't being followed. "MacLeod would have to be psychic to find us," he said.

"We'll soon know. Turn right here and follow this street to its end."

He did as she directed and soon saw the gleam of water ahead.

"Now turn left," she said, her voice hardening and the Lilliput appearing in her hand. "We're a block from the inner side of Crescent Harbor, and we're going to the outer rim."

They passed a watchmaking factory and a cluster of electronics plants whose products were in such demand that full night shifts were at work. At each corner Douglas caught a glimpse of freighters and small tankers tied up at docks. The odors of burning oil mingled with a strong smell of rubber, and clouds of low-lying smog formed a blanket that concealed the night sky.

"This is the road," Eleanor said, peering out at a street sign. "Follow it to the harbor."

Douglas slowed to a crawl. A warehouse stood on the left, a plant that manufactured television cabinets occupied the entire area on the right and at the end of the road a concrete wharf jutted out into the water.

The broken windshield partly obscured Eleanor's view, and she leaned out of the window to inspect the scene. A small freighter was berthed on one side of the wharf, and several small boats that bobbed up and down in the water were tied up on the other.

"Drive right onto the dock," she said.

Experience was making him cagey, and he hesitated. "If we do it won't be easy to pull out in a hurry."

"That won't happen," she said. "No one has followed us, so this is the end of the road."

He drove onto the wharf, parked near the outer end and switched off both ignition and headlights. "Now what?"

Eleanor gestured, and they climbed out of the truck. Two sampans were docked side by side, and she inspected them with care, relaxing visibly when she saw a cluster of green and red pennants flying from the nearer mast. A light beneath the canvas canopy indicated that someone was on board the craft.

"Wing Ah's lieutenant is waiting for me," Eleanor said in a low voice. "His guards are on the other sampan. Everything is just as Wing said it would be. Wait for me here, Doug, and keep an eye on the truck. This should take only a few minutes—just long enough to count the money and the securities." She walked to the side of the dock and whistled four times.

An answering whistle sounded from within, and a man wearing a coolie hat that concealed his face appeared in the stern. He extended a hand, and Eleanor climbed down into the sampan, disappearing with him into the interior.

Douglas lighted a cigarette, throwing the match into the harbor, which was laden with industrial debris. Escape from Hong Kong had seemed impossible earlier in the day, but Eleanor appeared to be on the verge of succeeding, and he wondered what kind of craft Wing Ah had agreed to give her.

The time for departure was at hand, but he realized that by fleeing with her he would be accepting the brand of a fugitive. If she could handle the boat alone it would be far better to turn himself in to Chief Inspector Li or Sir Frederick Simpson and offer a full explanation of all that had happened. It occurred to him, now that he was calmer, that he could offer a strong, legitimate plea of self-defense in the incident that had resulted in the death of the criminal who had wanted to kill him. It was probable that he would be acquitted, and the only permanent damage would be the harm to his reputation that would linger after he faced the initial barrage of publicity.

That, however, was a relatively small price to pay, and was far less costly than being labeled by the authorities as Eleanor's accomplice, which would be sure to happen if he left Hong Kong with her in a boat. He would try to persuade her to see his position through his eyes, and they could arrange to meet later in Central America or Brazil, after she settled there and he resumed his practice.

Suddenly someone crashed into Douglas from the rear, toppling him to the concrete, and the force of the unexpected assault was so great that he was almost knocked into the water. In order to avoid sliding into the oily sea he instinctively grappled with his attacker, and found himself staring into the cold, pale eyes of a sandy-haired giant.

The man's thick fingers closed around his victim's throat before Douglas could utter a cry for help.

It was evident that the brute knew his business, and Douglas realized that in less than a minute he would strangle. He was in good physical condition, but his strength was no match for that of his attacker, who had also utilized the element of surprise to gain an advantage.

Rather than claw at the hands that were systematically choking him Douglas knew he had to find a more immediate and effective means of escape. Only his knowledge of human anatomy saved him. Reaching up with whatever reserves of ebbing strength he could muster, he pressed his thumb into a nerve in the man's shoulder.

The counterattack in no way incapacitated the giant, but his hold loosened for a moment.

Douglas used the brief respite to draw air into his lungs, and with his other hand he dug hard into the side of his attacker's neck, just below the ear.

The man grimaced.

Douglas pressed still harder, knowing that no one could tolerate the excruciating pain for long.

The giant released his tormentor, then tried to remove the hand that was causing him such exquisite torture.

Desperation renewed Douglas' strength, and using all the force he could muster, he drove his knee into the man's groin.

The giant doubled over.

Douglas rolled free and scrambled to his feet. An all-consuming hatred enveloped him, and he no longer thought of shouting for help. As he fought for breath his one overwhelming desire was to inflict punishment on the brute.

The giant recovered quickly, and he, too, leaped to his feet.

The sight of the man's enraged face cooled Douglas' temper, and he knew he would need more than physical strength to win a battle in which neither combatant could expect quarter.

If the assailant had used common sense he would have realized that the odds in his favor were enormous, but he reacted like a maddened beast. Both arms thrashing wildly, he lunged forward.

Douglas waited until the last possible instant, then side-stepped, aiming a sharp kick at the groin of the onrushing giant.

The blow landed on target with a sickening thud, and the man crumpled to the concrete.

It did not occur to Douglas that his judgment was impaired. No longer caring about his safety, he threw himself at the giant, and his fists crashed repeatedly into the rawboned face. He heard a snapping sound that told him he had broken a nose bone, but the knowledge rekindled his own fury, and he continued to rain blows on the prostrate man until his knuckles ached.

Then powerful legs caught him in a vise-like grip and he felt himself being lifted into the air, then thrown to the wharf.

A knife appeared in the giant's hand, and he raised his arm to strike.

Once that huge hand began its downward sweep, Douglas knew, it would be impossible for the man to miss his target. Pinned to the concrete now, Douglas realized that only one chance remained, and catching hold of the upraised wrist, he pressed his fingers as hard as he could into the nerve on the inner side.

The giant's gasp was explosive, and the knife clattered to the dock, landing a few inches from Douglas' side.

Before the man could pick it up again Douglas managed to catch hold of it and flung it into the sea. Now they would fight on more equal terms.

Again the pain-crazed assailant reached for his victim's throat, and again Douglas' hand pressed into the side of his neck. Strength seemed to flow into the surgeon's fingers, and the man opened his mouth to scream, but was unable to utter a sound.

Determined to keep the upper hand at any cost, Douglas maintained all the pressure he could summon, and when the man went limp the American threw him onto the concrete, climbed onto his chest and used his knees to immobilize both powerful arms.

Catching hold of the giant's hair, Douglas lifted his head, then smashed it backward against the concrete, repeating the violent gesture until he grew weary.

"That's enough! Stop, Doug!" Eleanor's voice penetrated Douglas' consciousness, and she seemed to be speaking from a great distance.

He glanced toward the sound and saw her immobilized in the grasp of a tall, slender man, who released her with an apologetic smile.

She leaped to the dock, with the man at her heels, and they were joined by two burly Chinese from the other sampan.

"I wanted to help you, darling," she said, "but Monsieur Gautier had more sense and wouldn't let me interfere."

Douglas turned back to peer at the still giant. Sightless eyes looked up at him from a bloody face, and he knew, even before taking the man's pulse, that his attacker was dead.

"You killed Larson," Eleanor said, and there was awe in her voice.

"Madame," Gautier said, "we cannot wait. MacLeod will send others to see how Larson fared, and no one will believe the doctor acted without help. MacLeod will think we were responsible, and there will be open war between the syndicates."

Eleanor helped Douglas to his feet. "Give me the keys to the back of the truck, Doug. Quickly!"

He stared at her blankly for a moment. One thought drove everything else from his mind: within a few hours he had killed two professional murderers.

"Please, Doug!"

He reacted at last, and was afraid he had lost the keys in the fight, but after fumbling he finally found them in a hip pocket.

Eleanor snatched them from him and unlocked the rear door of the truck.

The combined efforts of Gautier and the two silent Chinese were required to move the keg from the truck to the farther sampan. The trio remained on board, and Gautier cast off. "Adieu, madame," he said. "You'll be wise to leave rapidly, also."

Eleanor guided Douglas to the remaining sampan, handing him a conical coolie hat and loose-fitting jacket, then donning a similar disguise.

He was still dazed, but his mind was beginning to function again. "It will take all night to pole a few miles," he said.

She untied the line, coiling it on the aft deck. "I think not," she said, and a powerful engine came to life when she pressed a button.

The sampan cut through the harbor filth and headed toward the open waters of the South China Sea.

XIX

A swallow of cognac and a brief rest in a bamboo chair on the aft deck helped Douglas regain his equilibrium, and as he watched Eleanor steer the sampan into the open sea with an experienced hand it occurred to him that she was knowledgeable in many fields. Her talents had been wasted, but it was not too late for her to begin anew and lead a law-abiding, useful life.

She became aware of his scrutiny, and her broad smile was an accurate reflection of her feelings. "Wing Ah did more than keep his pledge," she said. "We have enough food, water and fuel on board for a week's voyage. Far more than we'll need."

Apparently she had a specific destination in mind.

"We're sailing to Malaysia," she said, replying to his unasked question. "We'll reach one of the little ports on the east coast without strain after no more than two days and nights."

Douglas realized he was truly a fugitive now, his plan to give himself up to the authorities irrevocably destroyed by his fight on the wharf with the syndicate strong man. Eleanor would place herself in greater jeopardy if he asked her to put him ashore on one of Hong Kong's islands, a request his conscience would not permit him to make because he would be condemning her to the difficult task of making her way alone. He had sworn, when he had taken his marriage vows, to cherish her for better or worse, but it had never crossed his mind that he would become an expatriate, an outcast who could no longer practice his profession.

"There are almost as many Chinese as there are Malaysians in those ports," Eleanor said. "I have connections with some of the prominent families, and they'll help us. You'll see."

"What kind of help do you have in mind?"

"We'd be too conspicuous if we went to Kuala Lumpur," she said. "Even though it's the capital now it still has a small-town atmosphere and everyone knows the business of everyone else. We'll do better in Singapore."

Eddie Baker, he thought, would have to find another partner; one surgeon could not handle the large practice alone.

"Before we reach Singapore," she continued, "we'll have new passports, new identities. We'll stay there for a while—as long as we must—until MacLeod stops searching for us and Interpol is distracted by newer and more important cases."

He would no longer be able to claim that forces beyond his control had been responsible for his predicament. By falling in with her scheme and voluntarily cooperating with her he was making himself her accomplice, and no explanation he might offer the authorities would convince them that he had agreed because there had been no choice.

"Eventually we'll go to Mexico," she said, "and by then we'll have decided whether we want to make our permanent home in Central America or Brazil."

Unable to feign enthusiasm, he could only nod.

They passed a tanker heading in the opposite direction, toward Hong Kong Harbor, and Eleanor maneuvered deftly so they wouldn't be swamped by its wake. "When we reach international waters," she said, "you can take the tiller and I'll get us something to eat."

"I'm not hungry."

"You'll need food if we're going to spell each other through the night, darling. Besides, we owe ourselves a celebration. I thought we were finished when Larson attacked you and Gautier wouldn't let me help you because he was so afraid his syndicate would become involved. Larson was such a terror that even Ian was a little afraid of him. I had no idea that you're so strong."

Neither now nor in the future would he willingly discuss the fight that had ended in his foe's death. Turning away deliberately, he looked out at Hong Kong's tree-covered outer islands, many of them uninhabited.

She fell silent, too, knowing that nothing she might say would improve his spirits. In time his natural resilience would reassert itself and he would learn to accept his vastly altered situation.

The sampan moved at a steady speed, and as the moon rose higher Eleanor steered a course between two tiny islands that lay less than a half mile apart. She was following the deep-water channel, she explained, because it was the shortest route to the south even though international traffic was heavier in these waters. Her one immediate desire was to leave Hong Kong far behind.

Even at sea, however, there was no isolation. They passed within hailing distance of several sampans returning to port after spending a long day of fishing, and ahead they could see the fantail of a battered freighter. Then a fishing junk putting out to sea began to overtake them, its diesel engine humming loudly.

Eleanor veered to starboard to allow the junk ample passage space in the center of the channel.

The master of the ship appeared to be in a playful mood, however, and followed the course set by the sampan.

"The idiot!" Eleanor became angry. "If he isn't careful he'll swamp us!"

The junk continued to bear down on them.

Eleanor edged still farther to starboard.

Douglas began to share her alarm, and when he looked up at several figures in the prow his heart sank. "I think," he said, "we'll have to postpone our celebration."

She drew in her breath. "Ian! I should have recognized his ship!"

The junk, sailing at a speed greater than the sampan could achieve, cut off the smaller vessel, forcing Eleanor to turn off her engine or destroy her small craft by ramming into the junk's thick hull.

Ian MacLeod and two other men loomed overhead, and the syndicate leader held a submachine gun cradled in one arm. He had won the battle of wits after all, Douglas realized, by closing in at the last possible moment.

MacLeod picked up a microphone that would amplify his voice. "Sorry to inconvenience you," he said, "but we're lowering a line to you, and you'll oblige me by making fast to it. No tricks, please! I've lost patience with you."

The trap had shut. Eleanor looked around wildly, realized that flight was impossible and composed herself. Her face became a mask of indifference.

A length of line dropped to the deck of the sampan, and a powerful searchlight beam almost blinded the couple on the little craft.

"Make fast!" MacLeod ordered.

Eleanor tied a secure knot, aware that every move she made was being watched.

"Now come on board!" MacLeod directed. "You first, Chang."

A rope ladder was lowered down the side of the junk.

Douglas helped Eleanor mount the first rung.

"We'll think of something," she told him, but her eyes were bleak.

A rifle and an automatic were trained on her as she climbed the ladder.

Douglas was afraid to think of what awaited her as she vanished over the side.

"Your turn, Doctor!"

Douglas grasped the ladder and began his ascent, trying not to think of the guns that covered him. When he hit the deck rough hands reached out to help him over the side, and then he was subjected to a thorough, professional search by a man who found his .32 and removed it.

An automatic was jabbed into Douglas' back, and he was forced to walk aft, his hands raised over his head.

MacLeod stood at the fantail, still holding his submachine gun under one arm.

It was small consolation to see Eleanor standing, unharmed, near the railing.

MacLeod waved Douglas toward the girl, and he joined her. "Let me see your hands, Doctor."

Douglas extended them and turned them over, noting for the first time that his knuckles were swollen and cut.

"You actually fought Larson. And beat him." There was wonder in MacLeod's voice.

Douglas shrugged.

"I underestimated your capacities, Doctor. I won't do it again. Chang, you'll save me time and bother if you'll tell me where you've hidden Wing's money on board the sampan."

Eleanor was silent.

"Some people never learn the principles of cooperation. A great pity." MacLeod sighed, then turned again to Douglas. "You surprise me, Dr. Gordon. I thought you knew better than to interfere in matters you don't understand. I'd know I wasn't welcome in your surgery, and nothing would persuade me to go there."

Douglas could think of no adequate reply, but it didn't matter. He and Eleanor had tried to abscond with funds received in payment for gold the syndicate regarded as its own property, and between them they were responsible for the deaths of three of the organization's members. So their own fate was not in doubt.

A stocky, balding man approached and addressed MacLeod in a Cockney accent. "Kim has searched the sampan, Ian, but he can't find the bloody money."

MacLeod was annoyed. "Well, Chang?"

Eleanor averted her face.

MacLeod controlled his anger. "Haul the sampan on board," he said, "and we'll take it apart plank by plank. Chang wouldn't have sailed without the cash. Move along!" he added. "I don't want to spend the night in this channel. I'm tired of holding my breath until we pass the twelve-mile limit and reach international waters."

The Cockney hurried forward, shouting orders in Cantonese as he ran.

"Chang," MacLeod said, "just to satisfy my curiosity, where have you been the past few days? We scoured the city for you, and so did the police."

Eleanor's smile was malicious as she broke her silence. "I'm surprised you didn't guess, although you couldn't have touched us. We lived in the Walled City."

"Of course." To Douglas' surprise, MacLeod was amused. "I often wondered about you and Kung Hsien."

"Ian!" the Cockney shouted. "The sampan is on board!"

"Good. Full speed ahead." MacLeod remembered Douglas' presence. "I'm afraid I can't offer you a drink this evening, Dr. Gordon. I make it a policy to keep my personal and business activities separate." He looked forward as someone else approached.

Daphne MacLeod drifted toward the fantail, resplendent in a silver and white caftan that would have been more appropriate at a cocktail party than on board a converted junk. She paid no attention to Douglas, but glared at Eleanor.

"Damn you!" she cried, and leaped forward.

Douglas caught a glimpse of metal, and realized she had drawn a knife from the folds of her caftan. Before he could intervene the two women were fighting, both of them clawing, scratching and kicking.

MacLeod used his submachine gun to wave Douglas back to the rail. "Don't interfere," he said. "This is a rare spectacle."

Douglas couldn't share his enjoyment, and was sickened by the sight of the furious women falling to the deck as they tore at each other's faces, hair and clothing.

Daphne's arms and legs flailed without ceasing, but she was no match for her younger, more vigorous opponent. Eleanor had not only knocked the knife aside, but seemed intent on permanently disfiguring her attacker.

"That's enough!" MacLeod shouted, and had to repeat the order before they obeyed him.

Daphne struggled to her feet, a trickle of blood running down her face. "I found out all about you and Ian!"

"Go below and stay there," her husband said, his tone conversational.

Daphne looked as though she would lunge at the younger woman again, but instead she burst into tears and ran off down the deck.

Eleanor's chin was scratched, but otherwise she looked unharmed.

"I sympathize with you, Dr. Gordon," MacLeod said. "I know how disconcerting it is when a man discovers his wife has been unfaithful to him."

Eleanor was unable to meet Douglas' gaze.

The revelation that her affair with MacLeod hadn't been imaginary stunned him, and the worst of the situation was that she had lied to him.

"I would have stopped your little brawl," MacLeod said, "but I knew Daphne is too inept to handle a knife. There's no need for her to interfere when the sharks will dispose of you two after we're far enough at sea."

Even now, Douglas thought, the Scotsman adhered to his principle of not dirtying his own hands.

The Cockney approached, his shirt sweat-soaked. "We can't find it," he said, "not a penny of it!"

"Keep searching," MacLeod ordered, and the man went forward again.

The junk trembled as it cut through the water at full speed.

Douglas was confused, and told himself it was too late now to learn the whole story of Eleanor's involvements. They would be thrown overboard before he could press her for an honest, complete explanation.

Suddenly two searchlights illuminated the deck of the junk, one from the port and the other from the direction of the prow, slightly on the starboard side.

MacLeod seemed startled.

Douglas saw two gray Preventive Service cutters bearing down on the junk. Both were ready for combat, with uniformed gunners manning howitzers on their foredecks.

MacLeod hesitated for no more than an instant before throwing his submachine gun overboard. "Stand to!" he ordered. "Prepare to receive boarders!"

Douglas looked at Eleanor, but there was no way of guessing what might be going through her mind. Her face was drained of expression, and her eyes were fixed on the farther reaches of the dark horizon.

The junk lost speed, and when she stopped an anchor was thrown overboard. The cutters came alongside, and two young officers led a swarm of uniformed Preventive Service men on board. The junk's crew knew better than to offer resistance, and soon the whole company, including a protesting Daphne, was herded into the fantail.

The prisoners were crowded close together, and Douglas found himself standing beside Eleanor.

But she edged away from him, avoiding physical contact.

The last to appear were Chief Inspector Li and Sir Frederick Simpson, to whom the young officers reported.

"All hands have been taken, sir," the senior of the pair said.

"Put a prize crew on board," Sir Frederick replied.

MacLeod stepped forward. "You have no right to board my ship without a search warrant, gentlemen," he said.

Li handed him a legal document. "I'm sure you'll find this in order."

MacLeod glanced through it, but was not impressed. "I demand that you release us and leave my ship. This court order specifies no charges."

"That was left to our discretion, MacLeod," Sir Frederick said. "I've waited a long time for you to step over the line, and you've finally done it. We've caught you on grounds far more serious than gold smuggling. I charge you with kidnaping Douglas and Eleanor Chang Gordon, as well as taking possession of their vessel on the high seas. Piracy."

MacLeod grew pale beneath his tan, but did not lose his nerve. "Suppose Mrs. Gordon refuses to testify?"

"Oh, but she will," Sir Frederick said. "We're holding her sampan as material evidence, and I'm sure she'll cooperate with us in the hope the court will give her a lighter sentence." He glanced for the first time at Douglas. "But even if she refuses Dr. Gordon can tell us enough to hang you."

MacLeod made a final, desperate effort. "I refuse to make any statement until I've conferred with my solicitor."

The officials were not surprised. "The best solicitors in Hong Kong can't save you this time," Li said. "And I believe your associates in London and Switzerland will break with you, too. You've finally gone too far."

MacLeod's composure cracked. "There's a fortune on the sampan," he shouted, "and it belongs to me!"

Sir Frederick shook his head, an expression of pity in his eyes. "No, MacLeod," he said. "You've been outsmarted. There isn't a penny on board that boat."

XX

Ian and Daphne MacLeod were handcuffed, as were members of their crew, and Chief Inspector Li supervised their transfer to one of the cutters.

Sir Frederick Simpson remained on the fantail of the junk with Douglas and Eleanor, standing between them. "Well, Mrs. Gordon?" He was showing unexpected compassion.

Eleanor's shoulders slumped. "I'll have no better way to fill my time, so I'll write a full confession. Is that what you want to hear?"

"I'm sure the court won't be ungrateful," Sir Frederick said.

She turned to Douglas. "I'm sorry," she said, "for everything. I tried to tell you about my affair with Ian, but I changed my story when I saw you were hurt. That was the least of it, though. Nothing worked out the way I planned."

Sir Frederick signaled to a junior officer. "She won't need handcuffs," he said. "She'll be a Crown witness."

Eleanor walked forward to the cutter, the junior officer beside her, and did not look back.

Sir Frederick cleared his throat. "You and I will sail back to Hong Kong with the prize crew, Dr. Gordon. I don't know about you, but speaking strictly for myself, I need a drink."

Douglas followed him to the junk's elegantly furnished cabin. The Deputy Commissioner of the Preventive Service was treating him like a gentleman, even though he was a prisoner, too, and he appreciated the gesture.

Sir Frederick mixed two strong drinks of Scotch and water. "You've given us several anxious days, you know."

"An apology," Douglas said, "would be too feeble."

The older man raised his glass in a cheerful salute. "Oh, I want no apologies. After all, my people are paid to keep watch over foreign bumblers who fall into messes they don't understand and can't possibly control. Neither you nor Mrs. Gordon knew it, but we've kept you under a strict surveillance ever since she took you off to the Walled City."

Douglas stared at him.

"We couldn't take unnecessary risks with the lives of our star witnesses, although I must admit you did give me a few frightening moments. Not that any of the recent developments could be helped, of course. We had to allow the crisis to develop as we felt increasingly positive it would."

Douglas sipped his drink, then massaged his sore knuckles. "I've had a long day, so I'm a little slow in putting the pieces together."

"Inspector Li and I have realized for a long time that once MacLeod was maneuvered into a corner he'd go too far. That he'd finally commit an overt criminal act and make it possible for us to nab him. You were the catalytic agent that set the wheels in motion."

"I still don't see how I've figured in all this," Douglas said.

Sir Frederick added another splash of whisky to each glass. "Brace yourself, and I'll begin at the beginning. Eleanor Chang was MacLeod's mistress for several years. Without his wife's knowledge. He broke off with her about a year ago, when he discovered she'd stolen a keg of pure gold ingots from him some months earlier."

"I've seen the keg," Douglas said.

The older man ignored the interruption. "They kept up a surface relationship, MacLeod because he was determined to regain possession of the gold, Chang because she was trying to work out a way to keep the gold and escape with it. She knew MacLeod wouldn't order her killed before he learned where she had hidden it. Finally she thought of you, the one person who could help her without hurting her."

Douglas leaned forward in his chair.

"Everyone else in her circle would have demanded a share of the gold. You were the only man who had no interest whatever in the money it would bring."

"Fair enough, but—"

"Hear me out," Sir Frederick said. "She felt reasonably certain she could keep you pretty well in the dark. But whatever you might learn about her schemes wouldn't matter. You were her legal husband, and consequently you couldn't testify against her in a Crown court. Your hands were tied from the moment she brought you racing to Hong Kong to act as her protector."

Douglas frowned. "I'm not arguing with anything you say, but there's one angle you haven't taken into consideration. Our personal involvement with each other came alive again."

"There's still a great deal you don't know, Dr. Gordon," Sir Frederick said in a quiet voice. "You became romantically involved with your wife again. She did not become involved with you."

"Now you've gone too far."

"Your quarters in the Walled City were bugged, and I hope you'll forgive the intrusion on your privacy that we considered essential. So I know far more than you realize. Mrs. Gordon understood you rather well, and she was relying on a rekindling of the romantic spark to cloud your judgment. Which it did."

Douglas was unwilling to accept the assertion. "I'll admit I haven't been too bright, but I'm sure she felt as I did."

"You're mistaken." Sir Frederick stood, wandered around the cabin and then sat again. "She had no intention of living with you in New York. She had no intention of setting up a home with you in Central America, Brazil or anywhere else."

Douglas drained his glass.

"Put yourself in her position," the older man said. "MacLeod, who was under pressure from his own bosses, was becoming more and more strident in his demand that she return the syndicate's gold to him. Chang knew that eventually he'd torture the truth out of her. Meanwhile the Preventive Service was breathing down her neck. We pushed hard. Deliberately, so she'd make a break. Which is precisely what she did."

"By sending for me?"

"You'll have to pardon my bluntness, Dr. Gordon, but you've been a handy helper and a convenient smoke screen, nothing more. The young lady needed far greater protection than you could offer her."

The cabin was air-conditioned, but Douglas was perspiring.

"Eleanor Chang Gordon is an exceptionally clever woman," Sir Frederick said, "and she proved it by going to the one man who could give her everything she needed. Wing Ah, of the Chiu Chow, a leader of a rival syndicate."

"I met him."

"To be sure. One of his guards in the New Territories walled village is a highly valued Preventive Service agent. Now, as I was saying, think of the offer as Wing Ah saw it. His syndicate would gain possession of gold worth almost seven hundred thousand American dollars. More than double that sum on the black market. And it would be turned over to him in a way that wouldn't involve his syndicate in a fight with MacLeod's people. He would also gain the full-time services of a young woman who had proved she was far more than a courier. She would join his brain trust in the Golden Triangle, where the security is so tight the MacLeod gang never could have penetrated it."

Douglas reached for the bottle of Scotch. "Then she wouldn't have flown to Mexico and on to Central America with me?"

"She planned to disappear soon after you reached Singapore, and you never would have seen her again." Sir Frederick's voice became gentle. "You see, she had also become Wing Ah's mistress. He found the combination of her many appeals irresistible."

Douglas pushed his drink away. "So there was never any money and negotiable securities on the sampan. That was a fairy tale strictly for my benefit."

The older man nodded. "I'm afraid so. Just remember she fooled MacLeod, too, the one person as clever as she herself."

For a long moment Douglas was silent, and there was no sound in the cabin but the throbbing of the junk's engine as it headed toward Hong Kong Harbor. Finally he straightened his shoulders. "Thanks for filling me in, Sir Frederick. Now I'll return the compliment and save the police a lot of bother. Early this evening a member of MacLeod's syndicate named Dorfman was run down by a truck. It was no accident. A few hours later another MacLeod goon named Larson was killed in a slugging match on a New Territories wharf. I was responsible for both deaths."

Sir Frederick tinkled the ice in his glass. "When you read tomorrow morning's newspapers you'll read that the police have already solved the murders of Dorfman and Larson. Chief Inspector Li states very specifically that they were killed in the syndicate war that has led to the capture of Ian MacLeod and Eleanor Chang Gordon, as well as a number of lesser fry. You'll also discover that you've been something of a hero in the entire affair. Your American newspapers are certain to print the story, so you may have to allow the press to interview you when you reach New York."

A Preventive Service limousine took Douglas to Kaitak Airport. From the Kowloon overdrive he could see the Walled City, but he deliberately looked the other way. It was only midmorning, he told himself, and by noon the heat would be unbearable. He hadn't acclimated to the heat after five days. He felt as though he had spent far longer than five days in Hong Kong.

Thanks to Sir Frederick he was granted the courtesy of the airport, and was taken directly to his waiting airplane, its jet engines already warming up. The doors were closed as soon as he seated himself, and the giant of the air taxied to the far end of the runway. Douglas closed his eyes.

When he opened them again and looked out of his window Hong Kong was far below, although he could still make out the towering skyscrapers and high-rise apartment buildings on both sides of the harbor. Off to his right lay the green stretch of the New Territories, and beyond were the ancient hills of China.

Soon he would be home, greeting Eddie Baker and Eve Harrell, resuming his practice and slipping back into familiar routines. But he couldn't think of Eddie and his practice—and especially Eve—just yet.

First he had to get the last vestiges of Eleanor out of his system. It wouldn't be easy, but he'd do it because he had no choice. And by the time he landed in New York he'd be ready for the life that awaited him.